Books by Elaine Ford

THE PLAYHOUSE

MISSED CONNECTIONS

IVORY BRIGHT

MONKEY BAY

LIFE
DESIGNS

LIFE DESIGNS

~

Elaine Ford

Z

ZOLAND BOOKS
Cambridge, Massachusetts

First edition published in 1997 by
Zoland Books, Inc.
384 Huron Avenue
Cambridge, Massachusetts 02138

PUBLISHER'S NOTE
This book is a work of fiction. Names, characters,
places, and incidents are either the product of
the author's imagination or are used fictitiously.
Any resemblance to actual events or persons,
living or dead, is entirely coincidental.

Chapter VIII appeared in different form in
Colorado Review as "The Rock as Big as the *Queen Mary*."

FIRST EDITION

Book design by Boskydell Studio

Printed in the United States of America

04 03 02 01 00 99 98 97   8 7 6 5 4 3 2 1

This book is printed on acid-free paper, and its binding
materials have been chosen for strength and durability.

Library of Congress Cataloging-in-Publication Data
Ford, Elaine.
Life designs : a novel / by Elaine Ford.
p.   cm.
ISBN 0-944072-80-1 (cloth : alk. paper)
I. Title.
PS3556.0697L54   1997
813'.54—dc21   97-3163
                                      CIP

FOR ARTHUR

———

With special thanks to
Professor Emeritus Jacob Bennett

LIFE
DESIGNS

I

1962

EVERY DAY Meg doubted she'd make it until six. Mostly on account of the smells — candies that seemed to have picked up the cheap perfumes from the makeup counter in the next aisle, potato chips radiating their greasy stink all over the store. After a week Meg was sure she'd gained weight from the smells alone. The uniform she'd been required to buy had fit okay when she first tried it on, but now felt too tight in her armpits and cut into her waist. Inside pink rayon she steamed like a sausage. Norm, the assistant manager, was always hanging over her counter, watching her scoop peanuts or jelly beans out of the glass cases and into paper bags. Did he think she was going to steal the disgusting junk if he didn't keep an eye on her?

On Friday, a few minutes before six, Norm herded the remaining customer, a grizzled old guy in mismatched clothing, out the front door. After she'd shut down her register Meg headed for the rear of the store with the other salesgirls.

Fran Gromek came out behind her. "Humid as hell," she said. "Taking the bus?" She began to walk along the street with Meg. "Me too. Car died yesterday."

"What's wrong with it?"

"I only paid fifty dollars for it. Could be anything."

The stop where you caught the Number 47 was a couple of blocks away, in front of City Hall. When they reached it, Fran sat on a bench and took a pack of cigarettes out of her grimy imitation leather handbag, which once had been white. "Smoke?" Fran asked.

"No thanks."

Fran lit up and said, "How do you like working at Woolworth's?"

"For a summer job it's all right."

A Number 116 pulled up. The hot blast of air from the bus's idling engine churned Fran's short permed hair, revealing brown roots. Something about sitting here with Fran made Meg uneasy. Though the girl lived on Musson Street, not far from Meg's house, and was in her class, she barely knew her. Fran had gone to St. Agnes's up to ninth grade, then into the commercial track in high school. Occasionally Meg had seen her standing at the window in the girl's john, smoking, looking out at nothing.

"I hate it," Fran said. "The old biddies think if they only can find the exact right shade of lipstick they'll turn into movie stars, like magic."

Meg watched a bus ticket that somebody had failed to return to the driver blowing around in the gutter.

"No magic in Woolworth's," Fran said, "take it from me. Even makeup was better than notions. I could murder Norm for sticking me in notions. You cut four yards of fabric for some dame and after you've got it all wrapped up, and the sales slip made out, she says in a goody-goody little voice, *Oh dear, I guess that color's not right for my den, after all.*" Fran flicked ashes onto the sidewalk. "So you tell her, look, lady, once it's been cut from the bolt you've bought it, store policy, no exceptions. And what does she do? She yells for the manager or puts the evil eye on you."

Meg couldn't imagine speaking to a customer that way herself, but she said, "I know what you mean."

Number 116 departed, having picked up only a couple of passengers. Across the street, a bald man came out of Solomon's Shoe Store, turned the key in the lock, and walked away. Though it wouldn't be dark for another two hours, a grainy dusk seemed to be gathering. Meg looked at her watch and wondered if for some reason this run of the 47 had been canceled.

Fran tossed her cigarette into the gutter and rooted around in her purse until she came up with a little black-handled penknife. With her teeth she opened the blade. Meg watched her scrape letters into the plank they were sitting on, lifting painted splinters out of the wood. F.R.G. "Frances Rae Gromek," she said. "I like leaving my initials places."

The 47 came, almost twenty minutes late. Fran hopped onboard, and Meg followed.

~

Late Monday night, when Meg's brother got home from working the three to eleven shift at the hospital, they had a cake waiting for him on the kitchen table. Spelled out in aqua script on white frosting: *Happy 18th Birthday Kevin.* Meg and her mother sang a ragged "Happy Birthday to You," and Kevin blew out the candles. "Cool," he said. "Now they can draft me."

Meg began to cut the cake. Their father took a handkerchief out of his pocket and blew his nose, thoroughly reaming each nostril before he spoke. "What else do you have to do with your life, Mr. Varsity Swim Team?"

Tag line for a well-worn argument. Why hadn't Kevin applied himself when he had a chance? Why hadn't he gotten decent grades like his sister, instead of splashing around in a goddamn swimming pool? As always, Meg felt like crying or running away with the gypsies. Sometimes it seemed to her that Kevin failed for no other reason than to spite his father.

Without replying, Kevin left his slice of cake on the plate, only one bite eaten, and went out the screen door. Their mother was collecting the birthday candles to save for the next birthday, her own, in November. "Why did you have to say that?" she asked. "Why did you have to spoil his birthday?"

"I suppose you think it's dandy he's going to empty bedpans for the next fifty years."

It's good Kevin likes to help sick people, Meg thought. Why can't he get any credit for that? Silently she got up from the table and started to clear. Rumble of thunder, or maybe the wind shifting to the west, bringing with it the hum of the expressway. In the kitchen she ate Kevin's slice of cake so it wouldn't just be shoved down the disposal or into the garbage.

~

"Look," Fran said, opening her purse and letting Meg have a peek inside. "I got one for you." Meg saw two shiny squares of cardboard, each with a pair of gold hoop earrings thin as wire attached. "The salary they pay, I figure they owe us."

Probably not worth much, Meg thought, or Woolworth's wouldn't be selling them. Still, stolen goods. Across the street Mr. Solomon was locking up. Today he wore a checked sports jacket in spite of the heat. "I don't have pierced ears," Meg said.

"I could pierce them for you." Fran tugged her fingers through straw-dry teased hair. Her face looked as though she'd scoured it with furniture-stripping compound, and her full lower lip might have been bitten by a wasp. She wasn't very pretty, not in any ordinary way. "All you need is a needle and a cork."

"I'm not sure I want pierced ears."

Without being invited, exactly, Fran got off the bus at Meg's stop. They found Kevin out front pushing the mower. Like bristles on a discarded scrub brush, dandelion stalks stuck up all over the trimmed part of the grass. He must have Tuesday off this week, Meg thought.

Kevin paid no attention to the girls as they walked past and climbed the steps to the back door. But later, after Fran had gone, he came into the kitchen and said, "Who was that?"

Meg stood at the sink washing up. Her earlobes, strung with dental floss to keep the holes from closing while they healed, hurt like crazy. She shouldn't have believed it when Fran said Meg wouldn't feel a thing. "Somebody from work."

Behind her, Kevin opened the refrigerator. "How come there's never any eggs in this house?" he complained.

"Maybe you'd like to take over the shopping."

He put a pan on the stove and lit the gas under it. He poured oil in the pan, took a hamburger patty out of a box in the freezer compartment. When the burger went into the pan, hot oil spattered over the stove, onto the flowered wallpaper behind, and on the floor. "I'm not going to clean up after that, you know," Meg said.

He put a couple of slices of bread into the Toastmaster. "I've seen her around school. Ugly as sin."

"Nobody asked for your opinion."

To do the mowing he'd taken off his tee shirt, and bits of cut grass clung to his skin. Like Meg, he sunburned easily. Also like Meg, his hair lightened from caramel to pale oak in the summer. When they were small, ladies in the market would take them for twins and gush over them, even though he was twenty-three months older. Now Meg's hair curled halfway down her back. He stood half a foot taller than she, with a swimmer's thickly muscled shoulders and chest.

The toast popped up. Kevin removed the patty from the frying pan and eased it onto one of the slices. Then he spread French's mustard on it. He'd never liked catsup, refused to eat anything with tomato sauce, including pizza.

"Where's Mom?" he asked.

"They went to look at dinette sets. Bradbury's is having a sale."

"We don't have a dinette."

"For the sunporch, Kevin. Where have you been?"

He arranged the second piece of toast on top of his burger and headed for the door. So her mother wouldn't complain about the mess when she got home, Meg sponged off the stove and the floor and, as best she could, the wallpaper. She washed the frying pan. Then she went upstairs to the bathroom. In the cabinet she found a bottle of alcohol and rubbed it well into both earlobes.

～

The next day shortly after 6:00 P.M. Kevin's car, a rusty red '55 Oldsmobile, materialized at the bus stop. Startled, Meg got up from the bench and opened the door on the passenger side. "What are you doing here?"

"Just happened to be passing by."

"Since when do you get two days off in a row?"

"Do you want a ride or not?"

Fran had already thrown her cigarette onto the sidewalk and was climbing into the rear seat. Before Meg quite got her door closed he'd pulled into the lane of traffic moving up Centre Street. "You didn't get fired, did you?" Meg asked.

Kevin said nothing. They passed the Plaza Theater, where people were already lining up to buy tickets for the early show. A big banner with icicles painted on it hung over the doors. They'd do a good business tonight, everybody dying to escape into air-conditioning.

"*Three Stooges in Orbit*," Fran said, reading from the marquee. "I wouldn't mind seeing that."

"Did you get fired, Kevin?" Meg asked.

"What is this, the Spanish Inquisition?"

Meg noticed a smear of ballpoint ink on the skirt of her uniform and wondered if she'd be able to get it out. Her ears throbbed. Infected, probably, in spite of half a bottle of rubbing alcohol.

They crossed the railroad tracks and at the blinker Kevin made the left turn onto Alcorn, a street of warehouses, secondhand car dealerships, appliance repair shops. The sun, low in the sky, reflected in plate glass windows and made them look like sheets of hammered gold. Kevin squinted, lowering his visor. Meg heard a match being struck, smelled sulfur, then smoke drifted toward Kevin's open window. For a mile or so they followed Alcorn, past the Dairy Queen where Kevin used to work, the elementary school Kevin and Meg had attended, an empty ball field. The cross on the roof of the Church of the Nazarene — lightbulbs screwed onto a metal frame — wasn't yet lit.

"I live on Musson Street," Fran told him. "Know where it is?"

"I know where everything in this town is."

"That's what you think." Fran's hands clutched the seat back. He must be able to feel her smoky breath on his neck. "It's the turn after Eddie's grocery."

When they got to her house, Kevin pulled up behind an ancient Dodge parked at the curb. Fran's dead car, probably. "Why don't you come in for a minute?" Fran said. "I could give you a soda or something." Suddenly Meg remembered hearing that Fran's father no longer lived with the family.

The house was a shabby one-story frame building next to a vacant lot filled with rubble. Meg knew Kevin wouldn't want to go in, and it was the last thing she wanted to do herself right now, with her aching ears and the ink stain on her uniform she had to try to get out. But she felt bad about the house, with its peeling asphalt siding that was supposed to look like tan bricks and instead just looked cheap. Fran might think it was because of her house if they refused to go in, so Meg said, "I could use a soda."

She and Fran got out of the Olds and started up the walk,

which wasn't paved, just a path worn between weeds. Dog poop beside it buzzed with flies. At first she thought Kevin was going to humiliate her by waiting in the car, or even worse, driving off, but then she heard his footsteps on the path. Maybe he was thirsty.

Behind the side door they heard barking. "My mom's not home," Fran said. "She works nights." Eventually, from the depths of her purse, Fran dug out a set of keys, and together they crowded into a dim entryway. "Shut up, hound," she said. The animal, a short-legged mutt leaking slobber from its jowls, nudged Kevin's jeans. "Don't mind him," she said. "Come on." The dog bolted down a flight of stairs, toenails scrabbling, tail thumping against drywall, and the three of them followed.

The basement area had been turned into a rec room — Ripplewood paneling, couch, television console on conical legs. Shriveled balloons from some long-ago party dangled from a nail that had been driven into the dropped ceiling. Had to be twenty degrees cooler down here, Meg thought. But dim and musty, with a faint odor of gas. Kevin noticed the stove behind the bar. "What do you cook?" he asked.

"Sometimes popcorn." Fran opened three cans of Pepsi. "When they tore down the house next door my dad salvaged the stove. The toilet, too, and the sink in the john. This was going to be our bomb shelter."

"After the bomb drops," Kevin said, "the gas and water mains will be busted."

"I guess he didn't think of that." She pushed their cans to them across the bar.

With a sighing wheeze the dog sprawled on linoleum, the speckled kind that wasn't supposed to show dirt but did anyway. Meg sat on the couch while Kevin wandered around looking at things: a cuckoo clock that had ceased to work, bowling trophies on a shelf, a framed landscape mounted at eye level on the dark

Ripplewood wall. He flicked a switch on the frame. Suddenly fluorescent light glowed from behind the glass, illuminating a lake and splashing trees with a feverish shade of red.

"My mom adores that picture. It's where she's going to retire to, she says."

"Where's it supposed to be?"

"I don't know, someplace out west I guess." Fran lit a cigarette. "She'd go berserk in a place like that."

Kevin went into the john, and they heard him pee. The toilet took forever to finish flushing, the water swirling around and around in the bowl as if the toilet were draining all the pipes in the house, the street, the entire neighborhood. When he came out he started looking through a bunch of Reader's Digest condensed books and rumpled magazines and boxes of games and jigsaw puzzles. "Everything you'd need," he said, "to entertain yourself after a nuclear explosion."

Ignoring his crack, Fran sat on a rag rug next to the coffee table, an ashtray in her lap, and began to talk to Meg about Norm the Worm, forever breathing down her neck. Kevin flipped through an issue of *Motor Trend* dated February 1957. Probably shortly before Fran's father took off.

After a while Kevin tossed the magazine back into the pile and opened a cardboard box that had a dragon on the cover. *Dominoes* the box said in fake Chinese writing.

"Wanna play?" Fran asked.

"I might." He brought the box over and spilled the pieces out onto the glass-topped coffee table. They also had dragons on them, carved in relief on the backs. "How does it go?"

Fran smiled a little, setting her ashtray with the cigarette in it on the table. She began to turn all the pieces facedown, so the white spots were hidden and only the dragons showed. Kevin sat on the floor across the table from her. "First you have to shuffle, like in cards." The gold hoops in her ears glinted, and Meg realized she'd forgotten about the pain in her own earlobes. "Are you in, Meg?"

"I'll just watch."

To herself, and to Kevin, Fran dealt seven pieces. Bones, she called them. The extra dominoes were the boneyard. You had to match the bones to one another according to the number of dots at either end, drawing from the boneyard whenever you didn't have a match in your hand. Before long Kevin and Fran had constructed a right-angled pattern on the glass: office buildings at night, Meg thought, remembering the time they'd driven to the Boston Garden to see a Celtics game. High-rises with haphazardly lit windows. Finally only two pieces remained in the boneyard. When Kevin reached for one of them, Fran seized his wrist. "You can't."

"Why not?"

"It's the rule."

"You didn't tell me about any rule like that."

"It's still the rule. The last two bones can never be drawn."

"But I can't move."

"You'll have to miss your turn then."

"The hell you say." His other hand made a grab for the domino, and she snatched that wrist, too. They yanked at each other across the glass tabletop, both of them grunting and laughing, and the domino pieces flew everywhere. Fran's ashtray, the butt in it still smoldering, crashed to the floor. The dog woke up and growled. Then Kevin yelled "Hey!" and Meg saw that Fran had cut him with her fingernail. Beads of blood oozed out of the scratch. For a second Meg thought he was going to hit her, but instead he got to his feet and said, "Come on, Meg. It's late."

∾

Meg waited for the roof to fall in on Kevin for losing his job, but nothing happened. Thursday morning her father went off to work, complaining about the heat. He said, "You can trust Tru-Trust for one thing. Not to splurge on air-conditioning for its employees."

"He thinks he's got it bad," Kevin muttered. "He should try the orthopedic ward at Memorial."

Her mother did the grocery shopping, attended her Friday book club meeting, took down the drapes in the living room and sent them to be dry-cleaned. To all appearances, Kevin worked his shift as usual.

Sunday morning Meg put on her bathing suit. On her way to the backyard she dropped a bag of garbage into the outside can and noticed, half hidden amid apple cores and empty tuna fish cans, a parcel clumsily wrapped in brown paper.

She unfolded one of the lounge chairs, arranging it in a patch of sunlight between the maple tree and the garage. Then she rubbed suntan lotion onto her skin and opened her paperback. Meg had read only half a page when it occurred to her that the bundle in the trash was around the size of a baby. A newborn baby.

Lately in *Life* magazine or someplace like that she'd seen pictures of what they called "seal babies," born with nubbins for legs and flippers for arms or no arms at all. Some had birth stains, like the mark of Cain, on their foreheads. According to the captions, twisted inner organs required multiple delicate operations. Photos showed toddlers wearing leather harnesses attached to stainless steel claws. You'd have to be a saint to raise a child like that, Meg thought.

She imagined a woman leaving the expressway and entering their neighborhood. A parcel is on the car seat beside her. She's been planning on burying the parcel in a spot she has all picked out, under a tree in a lot that doesn't seem to belong to anyone. But the dirt turns out to be hard as concrete, and a dog comes sniffing to see what she's up to, and as the sun rises the traffic on the street grows heavier. Somebody's going to see her. Desperate to be rid of her burden, the mother gets back into her car and, weeping, thrusts the bundle into the first garbage can she finds.

Shade crept over Meg's spot on the lawn. She got up to shift the lounge chair and looked at the metal trash can. A homely and ordinary object, dented from being thrown to the ground by sanitation men, rust streaked and powdered with oxidation. Now, though, the can seemed menacing, a bomb about to explode. Forget it, she told herself. Leave it be.

But something made her go to the can and lift the ill-fitting lid and dig the parcel out. It was tied with twine and stained with spots from the garbage. The package didn't feel heavy enough to have a baby inside. Still, a dead one might weigh less than a live one, its bodily fluids evaporated, its bones gone soft and jellylike.

Forget it. Shove it back under the apple cores and forget you ever saw it.

In bare feet, the grass cutting into her soles, Meg carried the bundle into the garage and placed it on her father's workbench, amid pliers and skeins of wire and pads of steel wool and various-sized screwdrivers. With a utility knife she sliced the twine and then opened the brown paper. Inside she found, wrapped tight as a mummy, a white cotton shirt and pants such as hospital orderlies wear.

∾

Meg knocked on his door, and when he muttered something unintelligible, turned the knob. He lay on the bed in his underwear, his hair mussed, his face in the crook of his arm. Dark in here, and stuffy — at least ninety degrees, no breeze. "Want to go over to the Y pool with me?"

"No."

"Come on, Kev. It's so hot."

"I'm not in the mood. Go with one of your girlfriends."

She pulled the cord to open the venetian blind and looked out the window. In the distance, behind telephone wires and television aerials, the lightbulb cross on the Nazarene church shone pallidly. "I found your hospital clothes," she said. "You did get fired."

He lifted his arm from his face and squinted as if it was painful to look at her. "What were you doing digging in the trash?"

"What happened, Kevin?"

He didn't answer, but she knew if she stood there long enough, waiting, he'd eventually tell her. Like a sudden invasion, a flock of grackles swooped onto the back lawn, pecked around in the grass, and as suddenly flew off again. At last he said, "I was turning this guy in a body cast. I had him balanced on his side, and as I was tightening the draw sheet, I lost control and he came down like a load of cement."

"Onto the floor? Did you kill him?"

"No, I didn't *kill* him, Meg. If I killed him, do you think I'd still be here? I'd be halfway to China by now."

She pictured her brother wandering in some remote craggy wilderness, dressed in rags, hair grown out into impossibly matted curls.

"He fell on the bed. Knocked the wind out of him, otherwise he seemed okay. But one more incident report and I'd be up the creek, so I asked him not to mention it to anybody. He said sure, buddy, don't give it another thought."

Meg picked up Kevin's bedspread, which lay in a heap on the carpet. He'd had the same spread since he was a kid, little airplanes woven into the design. When he grew up he was going to be a pilot, he used to say.

"Monday that was. On Tuesday I'm in there taking his blood pressure, and he tells me he feels this pain now, whenever he takes a deep breath. He's nervous the fall wrenched something out of place, maybe cracked a rib, and it's not going to heal right. I had to tell the charge nurse, what else could I do? The next thing I know, I'm out on the street in that stupid monkey suit."

"Where's the clothes you wore to work?"

"In my locker in the hospital basement. I'm not going back for them, either."

"Oh, Kev." She dropped the spread in a heap onto the foot of his bed. "Dad's gonna blow a gasket when he finds out you got fired."

"I thought I'd find another job before I said anything. But Dairy Queen's not hiring, and they pay shit anyway. I tried some other places, no dice. Finally I applied to bag groceries at the Stop 'n' Shop, figured I'd start small and work my way up. The manager calls the hospital personnel office while I'm standing there. When he hangs up he says, 'Sure I'll give you a job — around the time pigs learn to fly.' "

Kevin had a positive gift, Meg thought, for stumbling into trouble that wasn't his fault. Well, not entirely his fault. "So now what?"

"Damned if I know," he said, pulling the sheet over his head.

∾

At the bus stop Fran opened her handbag, took out a new-looking lipstick tube, and removed the cap. A pale, almost white color, shiny as varnish. She spread a layer onto her lips and sucked them together. Meg knew she'd stolen it, but didn't say anything. "Want to come over to my house?" Fran asked.

"I can't. I've got things to do."

"Well, I'm probably going to be busy, anyway. Know what I mean?" she asked with a sideways little smile and an elbow in Meg's rib.

"Sure," Meg said, although she had no idea.

Two Number 156s pulled up and took off, one right after the other. Dropping the lipstick back into her purse, Fran said, "I've pretty much decided not to go back to school in September."

"What'll you do instead?"

She tucked her bra strap into her sleeveless blouse. "Oh, maybe go on working at Woolworth's for a while. I don't know, I'll think of something."

The 47 bus came, and when they'd slid into seats in the back Fran started talking about the nuns at St. Agnes's, how mean they were. They'd whip you if you broke any rules, even the tiniest of infractions.

～

June had been sunny and humid and hot. July was overcast and humid and even hotter. Rain vaguely threatened but mostly didn't fall — heat lightning instead. Potato chip molecules sank into Meg's hair and pores, through her otherwise impermeable rayon uniform, into the fibers of her slip and bra and panties.

She considered telling Norm she didn't feel well and escaping to the afternoon show at the Plaza. *Hell Is for Heroes* with Steve McQueen was playing. "Guys are suckers when you hint you've got the curse," Fran had said. "The subject spooks them so much they let you go without an argument."

But Meg couldn't quite bring herself to lie, or to approach Norm, either.

Kevin didn't tell their parents about losing his job. He'd be gone in his car by the time Meg got home from work and not get in until eleven-thirty or later. Meg figured he must spend the time playing one-on-one basketball with one of his jock friends or maybe swimming in endless circles at the Y, like a guppy in a tank. She couldn't embarrass him by asking, and didn't really want to know, anyhow.

One morning in early August, Norm slouched over to the food counter and said, "Where's your pal?"

"Who?"

"Gromek. She didn't bother to call in sick and don't answer her phone. I had to pull Sheila from handbags and put her in notions. Now handbags ain't covered."

That's your headache, Meg thought. She felt one of her own coming on. Outside it was pouring, looked like it was planning to rain all day.

"If you see her, tell her she better pull up her socks, or she can kiss this job good-bye."

"I'll tell her," Meg said, trying to unhitch her hair from the gold wire in her ear.

When she left the store at closing time rain still fell in a relentless drizzle, and by the time she got to City Hall her shoes were soaked through. On the bus, she thought about Fran. Maybe she really was sick, too sick to go to the phone.

Only a couple of cars were parked at the Dairy Queen. The ball field had turned into a muddy sea. They hadn't lit the cross on the Nazarene Church. In a last-minute decision, less out of resolve than a failure to get out of her seat and lurch toward the door, Meg stayed on the bus past her stop. She might as well check on Fran, make sure she was all right.

Musson Street looked every bit as dismal as it had the day Kevin gave them a ride home and he and Fran played dominoes in the basement. Maybe more so. Sodden newspapers had joined the other trash in the vacant lot next to Fran's house. Under her umbrella Meg walked up the path. Rainwater dropped from the low roof, landing on a few hosta plants struggling to survive amid ragweed and unmowed grasses going to seed.

Around at the side of the house Meg pounded on the door. The dog began to bark, but otherwise no response. Just as well, she thought. Insane idea, imagining Fran needed or wanted any do-gooders barging in on her. Meg was halfway up the path when the door opened and Fran called her name.

Reluctantly she walked back to the house. She went inside and they stood in the entryway, Meg's collapsed umbrella dripping onto her rayon uniform and her shoes. Fran's hair stuck out from her head in weird uncombed bunches, and her breath smelled of cigarette smoke. In some other part of the house, evidently shut in, the dog went on barking. "He told you, didn't he," she said. "I might have known he'd go blabbing to you."

"Norm? All he said was —"

"I'm not talking about Norm, for crimminy sakes. Your brother."

Confused, Meg stared at her. Fran's wrinkled pajamas gaped open, unbuttoned, revealing a breast hardly bigger than a child's fist. Behind her back Meg felt dank chill seeping up from the basement. "What's my brother got to do with anything?"

"Why are you playing dumb? You knew about him and me."

"I didn't, I swear." Meg thought she might topple backward down the stairs.

"You said you did. That day at the bus stop, the day I talked about quitting school."

"I didn't say any such thing. You're crazy."

"Crazy?" Fran yelled, about two inches away from her face. "Well, maybe I am, but I'm also pregnant."

No no no no

"A little Kevin growing inside me."

～

Kevin seemed to have shrunk, clothes and all, in the rain. How small his sneakers looked — she doubted they'd fit on her own feet. He picked up a twig, scraped inscrutable marks in the mud by his lounge chair.

Meg leaned back in hers, feeling the damp of the canvas seep through her shirt, and closed her eyes. A seal baby. Meg couldn't get the image out of her head. A seal baby with a bloody mark on its forehead and flippers instead of limbs.

"What am I going to do?" Kevin asked, desperation in his voice. She heard the end of the stick snap off.

He could not explain to Meg why he'd gone down into Fran Gromek's basement night after night. She wasn't pretty, he didn't even like her much. After the first few times, he confessed, he found her more pitiful than exciting.

But for hours he'd sit in his car, maybe parked in the lot behind the sanitation department, or at the elementary school, or at the Dairy Queen, listening to music on the only station the radio was strong enough to bring in. Then, late in the day, without any conscious thought in his head, he'd start the engine and drive to Musson Street. Follow her down the basement stairs, wrestle with her on the couch while the mutt sniggered through its nose and drooled onto the linoleum.

"I was never there for long," he said, as if that made any difference. "Half hour, hour at the most. It didn't mean anything, right?" No, he never thought of rubbers, never took what was going on that seriously. "Each time, I figured it was the last. If you go to the drugstore and buy yourself a packet of Trojans, that means it's serious."

"Don't kid yourself," Meg said. "It's serious."

~

More than a week went by. A new girl appeared in notions. Every day Norm would find some excuse to mention Fran's name, slyly grinning at Meg over her counter as if taunting her.

Constantly Meg tortured herself by trying to think how she could rescue Kevin from the pit he'd fallen into. If only she hadn't worried about hurting Fran's feelings, if only she hadn't agreed to stop in at her ratty little house for a soda, if only Kevin hadn't been with her.

Though Sunday was supposedly Kevin's day off, he didn't show up in time for supper. While Meg was doing the dishes he came in and walked through the kitchen without saying anything. After she finished scrubbing the last pot and dumped out the dishwater, she went upstairs. At his door she asked, "Are you hungry? Shall I make you a sandwich? There's some pot roast left over."

"No, thanks." He lay on his bed, listening to a Red Sox game on the radio.

"What's the score?"

"They're getting clobbered. Douse it, will you?"

She switched off the radio and noticed, amid the junk on his desk, a single domino. She turned it over and saw the dragon incised on its back.

"Why did you take this?"

He didn't answer.

"Now the set is ruined," she said stupidly. What did it matter?

Kevin got off his bed and walked to the window. The days are getting shorter, Meg thought. Only eight o'clock, and the sky already dark. The lightbulb cross glimmered through mist. "One dumb mistake," he said, his voice flat, "and your whole life goes down the drain."

"Have you talked to her?"

In the living room below, the television was on, a confused mumble pierced now and then by shrieks of laughter.

"I have to marry her, she says."

Rockabye baby if the bough falls down will come baby cradle and . . .

"If only," Kevin said, "that guy hadn't driven his bike into a wall."

Bike? She felt as if she'd come in after the movie had already begun. "What guy?"

"The moron in the body cast," he said impatiently. "The one I dropped. Drove his goddam Harley straight into a brick wall, and he wasn't even wearing a helmet. How could he have been so dumb?"

Loose threads were springing out of Kevin's old bedspread, ready to catch on something. If you didn't watch out the whole thing might trail after you, unraveling, attached to some button or snap or buckle.

"By rights he should've been in the morgue instead of —"

The telephone began to ring. Meg went to the phone in the hall and lifted the receiver. "Hello?"

"It's me. You better come over."

"Now? It's late. I have to —"

"Just come," Fran said, and hung up.

Meg got her purse from her room and stopped by Kevin's on her way to the stairs. He was still standing by the window, staring out into the dark. "I'm going over to Fran's," she told him.

"Is something wrong?"

"I think so."

For a moment they looked at each other. "I'll go with you," he said and pulled on his Keds and tied the laces.

"You don't have to."

He just shook his head, as if to clear his ears of water after a dive.

Outside, the air had a softness to it. Dew that quickly clung to you like a slimy outer layer of skin. Meg headed for the Olds in the driveway, but Kevin said, "It's out of gas."

"Oh, Kevin, why can't you ever —"

"I don't have a dime for gas or anything else."

Without saying anything more they began to walk to Musson Street. On Alcorn all you could see of the houses were bluish will-o'-the-wisps shimmering in downstairs windows. Crickets made sad music in scrubby patches of lawn.

Gradually the neighborhood became more run-down, zoned for commercial: a grubby mom-and-pop on a corner, a dry cleaner, several boarded-up houses, one of which had burned, initials scrawled on fences and the sides of buildings. It would not have surprised Meg to see F.R.G.'s among them.

Meg took comfort in the steady sound of Kevin's soles connecting with the pavement, the instinctive matching of his pace to hers. She wished this silent walk could go on forever, and not just because of what they might find at the end of it.

But they passed Eddie's grocery, closed now, and rounded the corner onto Musson. At Fran's house Kevin took a key out of the back pocket of his jeans, fit it in the lock, opened the door. The dog was right there, set to spring on them. With a hard jab of his knee Kevin knocked it out of the way. Dim light emerged from the stairwell. He started down the steps, and Meg went after him. The dog sat in the hall, whimpering.

What Meg saw first was blood on the linoleum. Then she saw Fran hunched against the far wall, her knees up under her chin. She wore the same thin summer pajamas, and they had blood on them, too, soaked in the crotch and down the legs. "Fran," Meg said. "What —"

"In the toilet."

As if moving under the weight of six feet of water, Meg went into the bathroom and turned on the light. Streamers of bloody membrane aswirl in the bowl, great clots like chunks of calf's liver. She didn't flush. Washing away all that gore would empty every pipe in the neighborhood, maybe the whole town.

When she came out she saw that her brother had lifted Fran onto the couch and raised her legs onto a bunched-up rag rug. Her face was chalk white and damp with sweat. "Kind of shocky," he said to Meg, his fingers on Fran's wrist. "Quick, go upstairs and call an ambulance."

In the hall at the top of the stairs Meg pushed past the slobbering dog and through a door. The house smelled sour, unaired. In a bedroom she found a phone and called the hospital, then ripped the sheet off the cot, leaving the mattress naked.

Back in the cellar, Kevin knelt by the couch, talking to Fran quietly.

"Act of God," Fran said in a half-laugh, half-sob.

Kevin tucked the sheet around her. "Do you want us to get in touch with your mother?" he asked.

"Christ, no."

"I think she's stopped bleeding," he told the emergency crew when they came. To Meg he said, "They'll take care of her. Let's go." His voice trembled. She saw tears in his eyes.

The next morning Kevin walked downtown to the recruiting station in City Hall and enlisted in the army.

II

1967

M EG RAISED the shade to half-mast. Through the open
window of their second-floor apartment came a hollow
keening sound, like air blown across the lip of a bottle. A mourn-
ing dove, she guessed, perched on some nearby eave or gutter.
The day would be a scorcher, she could tell already. For a moment
she stood watching Jim sleep, his mouth sagging open a little, his
arm flung into the space she'd just vacated. She laid her hand on
the gently swelling mound of belly under the old tee shirt she
used for a nightgown. Then she left the bedroom and went down
the hall to the kitchen.

Crowding the inside of the refrigerator were ten six-packs of
beer and three bakery boxes. She took out a quart of milk and
opened a box of corn flakes.

Meg carried the cereal bowl out to the back porch and sat on
the ancient iron glider that took up most of it. The springs
squealed; her bottom stuck to the cracked plastic cushion. Idly
she wondered how the landlord, or whoever put the glider there,
had managed to get it up the rickety back steps and over the rail-
ing — and why it didn't crash through the rotting floorboards
and land on the ground-floor porch below. Perhaps it would, one

day. The corn flakes had gone soft in muggy August weather, but she made herself eat.

Down in the yard that backed on theirs, on the other side of a high wood fence, a woman was hanging out her wash. She bent to the basket and flipped out a shirt or pillowcase before pinning it to the line, moving as though she were arthritic or had a lame hip. Her reward would be smelling the freshly aired clothes when she brought them in.

For the first time Meg regretted that she and Jim had not invited their parents to be here today. When they'd made the decision, it had seemed clearly the right one. "What benefit could there be," Jim had asked rhetorically, "in importing my folks from Dayton to raise holy hell?" Or, she'd thought privately, in subjecting herself to her parents' flustered dismay. But Meg hadn't counted on how lonely she would feel this morning. And scared. If only Kev were here. The irony was, if Kevin were here she wouldn't be.

～

On a miserable afternoon the previous February, after her Milton tutorial, she'd ridden her bike back to the dorm in unrelenting drizzle. *Down rushed the rain impetuous, and continued till the earth no more was seen.*

Along with her mail in the pigeonholes by the bells desk she found a slip of paper with the message that her mother had telephoned earlier in the day. Weird. Unlike her mother to call rather than write, and especially when the rates were highest, at that. She wondered what could be wrong at home. Maybe her grandmother was in the hospital with diverticulitis again. Or — Meg's constant fear over four years — her parents hadn't been able to scrape together the money for her tuition bill, and the Class of '67 would graduate without her.

Meg went upstairs to her room and changed her clothes. Stalling, unwilling to hear the news, she dried her long hair, untangling the knots the wind had driven into it. She filed a snagged fingernail and ate an apple right down to the core before dragging the communal phone on its long extension cord into her room and shutting the door.

Her father picked up the phone. Meg did not know how to defend herself against his blunt words: *Land mine. Never knew what hit him.*

"There's no" — her father cleared his throat — "no body. Meg?"

He waited for her to say something, but she couldn't get the words out.

"The memorial service will be on Friday. Your mother wants to get it over with. Do you need anything?"

"No," she heard herself say, "I'm okay for money."

She hung up and looked out the window at rain dripping into puddles on the quad. Not Kevin, it was not possible. Medics don't get killed, everybody knows that. Her brother's string of bad luck had turned when he joined the army. His letters to her were cheerful, confident. He liked the job he was doing, thought helping his wounded buddies was worthwhile. Never did he sound as if he was screwed up, or was scared he wasn't going to make it home.

How stupid to have worried about something as trivial as graduating with her class. Gladly she'd give up the diploma, even condemn the sour old lady to perpetual diverticulitis, if it would only save Kevin.

Maybe, she thought desperately, the army got the names confused. Maybe he'll turn up the way Jocko did, days after they'd given up scouring the city for him. The dog just barked at the door one day and calmly trotted into the kitchen looking around for his kibble bowl, which they'd put away because they couldn't stand seeing it anymore. Jocko died of old age when Kev was thirteen and Meg eleven. The family never had another pet, though. "You get too attached to them," her mother said. "They break your heart. It's not worth it."

∾

Meg stood at the sink peeling hot boiled potatoes. Jim came into the kitchen and helped himself to coffee from the percolator on the stove. Then he lit a cigarette. "Cooking already?" he asked. She inhaled his warm masculine smell along with the faintly rancid garbage pail, the metallic overheated coffee, the first puff of smoke.

"Potato salad," she said.

She still felt shy with him, especially in the mornings. She knew better now than to invite him to have some breakfast. Coffee — black — and a cigarette was breakfast for Jim.

He sat at the big oval table by the windows and unfolded the *Globe*, which she'd earlier retrieved from the downstairs hall. The front-page stories were about a bridge near Saigon blown up by guerrillas and race riots in New Haven. Sunlight gleamed on Jim's pale straight hair.

"Don't forget you have to mow the grass in the backyard this morning," she said.

"I'll get to it."

"Better not wait too long. It's going to be really hot today."

"Uh-huh," he said absently.

∾

The memorial service was in the church where she'd sung in the choir for seven years, where on a dare Kev had once tied balloons to the twenty-foot-high brass chandelier and nobody ever figured out how he did it. Now she would never know, ever. The thought set Meg off again. She wept until her eyes were swollen, her face chapped from salty tears.

The next day she went to an animal shelter and chose a puppy for her mother. Adorable little thing, orphan, runt of the litter. Her mother made her take it back. "Dogs tie you down too much," she said. What she wanted to be free for, Meg couldn't understand.

When she got back to school she was too distracted to take in what she read of Milton or Huizinga or Hardy or St. Thomas Aquinas. Often she failed to make it to the dining room in time for meals, existing on food she could buy from vending machines in the dorm basement. Sleep eluded her. Even when she'd finally lose consciousness at two or three in the morning, exhausted, she'd find herself buried alive in a slime of rotting body parts, twisted metal, slivers of bone.

Upheaval surrounded her, even in the safety of the dorm. Talk of draft card burnings, blood poured on the steps of recruiting stations, bombing raids, Black Power. Some days she never changed out of her pajamas or combed her hair.

Instead of going to class Meg played bridge on the third-floor lounge with girls she'd scarcely known before Kevin died, the outcasts and misfits. Alicia, who stuttered so badly she was almost unintelligible; Zoë, who'd been raped at the age of nine and never gotten over it; Yung-Ja, horribly homesick for Korea.

She thought of ending her life. She imagined plunging a knife into her heart, or blowing her head off, or taking the subway to Revere Beach and walking into the sea the way Virginia Woolf had done — or had that been a lake? But Meg knew she didn't have the guts to go through with any of those things. She didn't have a knife sharp enough, didn't know how to load or fire a gun. As soon as the seawater got into her nose she'd be gulping for breath, struggling to escape. If she did die it would be by dumb luck.

Day after day Meg went on playing bridge, as if the way the cards fell out might reveal to her some orderly and reliable pattern to life. Yet she hardly noticed whether she and Yung-Ja won or lost.

In the third week of March came hour exams. Within ten minutes she'd write down in her blue book whatever she knew about
the subject at hand and spend the rest of the period looking out
the window at the patterns bare branches made against a blank,
colorless sky.

Early in April her section man in Chaucer, Mr. Mowbry, summoned her to his office, a damp little cubicle. She sat on the
straight-backed chair next to his desk, waiting for the ax to fall.
"I'd like to know," he said, his mussed pale hair falling across his
brow, "why you are hell-bent on failing my course."

Idiotically, she began to cry. In embarrassment he cast about
among the objects on his desk for a box of tissues. "Is something
troubling you?" he asked kindly. "Why don't you tell me about it?"

Through her tears she explained about Kevin, her only
brother, dying somewhere in the Mekong delta. What was the
point of learning facts and dates when at any moment something
crazy could happen to you like stepping on a land mine?

"That's not very sound logic," he said. "What if you *don't* step
on a land mine?"

"Then it will be something else."

"Tell you what," he said. "Let's go have a cup of coffee."

In his beat-up VW they drove to a tiny place in Central Square,
and he ordered strong, sweet coffee in miniature cups. The sleeve
of his tweed jacket brushed her arm when he brought her a
pastry filled with almonds.

Later, in the dorm, she smelled his cigarette smoke in her
clothes. He'd offered to help her catch up in Chaucer. "Catch up?
It would pretty much be starting from ground zero."

"We could do that," he'd replied.

❦

From the yard came the smell of crushed, mowed grass and the
rattling sound of the landlord's hand mower, an occasional

growled oath when a rock or twig jammed the blades. Meg took the cake boxes out of the refrigerator and cut the strings. This would be easy, she'd figured. Buy three cakes frosted in plain white icing at the bakery and a plastic bride and groom in Kresge's, and assemble the cake herself. Almost as good as a real one and noticeably less expensive. She was determined that this occasion make no dent in their bank accounts.

She lifted the biggest cake out of its box and maneuvered it onto the center of the plastic platter she'd also purchased at Kresge's. The platter was supposed to look like cut glass. Some icing had come off onto her fingers, and she licked them. Sickly sweet, perfumed with artificial vanilla.

She was just easing the middle-sized cake onto the first one when the telephone began to ring. This caused her to set the cake down less gently than she'd planned, and also somewhat off-center. Terrific timing, she thought, wondering whether she'd be able to adjust the layer without altogether wrecking the icing. She went into the hall and lifted the phone.

"Have I reached the Mowbry residence?" asked the voice in the receiver. "Veekay here." Veekay Chatterjee, ABD (all but dissertation) in philosophy, was a roommate of Jim's from undergraduate days, who happened to be in town for the summer. "I am in Pioneer Budget Liquor Mart," Veekay went on. "The proprietor is wanting to know whether it is imported or domestic you are requiring."

"Whatever's cheaper."

"Very good. I will be arriving shortly."

Back in the kitchen, Meg saw that the middle cake had sunk, somewhat tipsily, about an inch into the first cake. Oh, no, she thought. Real wedding cakes must be made with a special batter that keeps them from doing that. Maybe this wasn't such a great idea after all. Sweat dripped down her back under her tee shirt. By now the temperature in the kitchen must be hovering at ninety degrees. Her forehead prickled at the hairline.

Be calm, Meg told herself. It is only a cake. It is not a matter of life and death. Fearing the worst, she lifted the third cake out of its box and placed it on the middle one. Luckily, this layer didn't sink quite so much. Meg ripped open the cellophane package that contained the bride and groom and planted them on top. The bride's painted black hair was very different from her own, but at least the groom had blond hair and blue eyes, like Jim's.

∼

Gingerly she took a seat on the threadbare sofa in Mr. Mowbry's living room. He removed a book from his attaché case and sat beside her. "I'll read a little out loud," he said. "So you can get the rhythms in your ear. For now, don't worry about the meaning.

"Whan that Aprill with his shoures soote
The droghte of March hath perced to the roote,
And bathed every veyne in swich licour
Of which vertu engendred is the flour;
Whan Zephirus eek with his sweete breeth
Inspired hath in every holt and heeth
The tendre croppes . . ."

Meg had begun to cry. It was so stupid, coming apart again in front of this kind young professor. Snuffling, she pulled a tissue from her pocket.

He paused. Acne scars in the corner of his mouth suggested to her that he might have other kinds of scars as well, internal ones. Perhaps he was a little less confident than he seemed.

"I'm sorry," she said. "I feel like such a jerk."

"Shoures soote," he whispered. Gently he touched her shoulder, awkwardly he fingered her long, curly, honey-colored hair. The book fell to the carpet.

Afterward he said, "I've never done this before. Not with a student. I feel good about it, and I don't think what we did was wrong, but I could get into trouble if —"

"I won't tell a soul."

Meg decided to clean the kitchen floor. She twisted her hair up off her neck and got the mop and pail from the porch. In the middle of the job Veekay came up the front stairs bearing a bottle of champagne in each hand. White bows affixed to their necks had gone limp in transit. "Thanks, Veekay," she said. "See if you can find room for them in the fridge."

"May I ask where is the bridegroom?"

"Mowing the lawn for the party. He should be right up."

The screen door banged and Jim came in the back way, shedding snips of grass and weed seeds onto the wet floor, his face a violent shade of red. He opened the refrigerator and tore a beer out of one of the six-packs. "Want one?" he asked Veekay.

"Thank you, no." He watched Jim pry off the cap and take a large gulp. "I have come to a decision," Veekay announced.

"What decision is that?"

"I am weary of waiting for other institutions to make up their minds. I am going to accept the offer from Calvary."

"You mean Calgary."

"No," Veekay said gloomily, "I mean Calvary."

Jim laughed. Meg wrung out the mop.

⁓

Almost every day around five o'clock Meg had skulked past the porter, hurried across the courtyard, and opened the door at E Entry. Up one flight of steps was the so-called suite allotted to Jim by virtue of his being a junior lecturer attached to the House — actually a sunless living room furnished with mismatched odds and ends left behind by previous generations of lecturers. When she got there he'd have a fire crackling in the fireplace, the sherry decanter on the coffee table. After an hour of reading to each other in Middle English, he'd give her a glass of sherry and take her to the little bedroom, and put her in his bed.

She loved how hungry he was for her body. She felt like a kind of magic food that could fill him again and again and yet never run dry.

"Margaret, Meggity, Meggie . . . Meg," he'd gasp during love-making, as if struggling to decline a noun in an almost-lost language.

Then he'd search through his rooms until he found a pack of cigarettes somewhere. He'd light one and sit up in bed with the sheet over his hips and talk to her about his summer plans: a trip to Bruges and Avignon, for which he'd been saving for years. Combined research and pleasure. On the way back he'd hit Oxford, too, scope out the Bod. Not too soon to begin zeroing in on a dissertation topic.

Lying in his bed next to him, Meg imagined going too. She pictured herself waiting for him in a medieval cathedral, gazing at ancient stained glass and statuary while he pored over manuscripts, and when he'd finished his work for the day they'd have a picnic in a meadow — red wine and cheese and crusty bread — and he'd make passionate love to her amid poppies and whatever other wildflowers grew in Belgium.

His lovemaking was beginning to change her body. Her breasts grew round and taut, as if bursting with milk, her nipples exquisitely tender to his touch. Her cheeks filled out, colored with the blush of ripening fruit. During lectures and tutorials she felt a firm pressure in her genital area as if he were inside her still.

Gradually her grief for Kevin had shifted from a leaden hopelessness to a bittersweet regret for what would never be. Now, she realized, her copious tears flowed for no reason at all.

One day at the mailboxes she encountered Alicia, who'd had to find another fourth for bridge now that Meg was no longer cutting classes. Alicia took a hard look at her and said, "B-b-by any chance are you p-p-p-pregnant?"

～

His feet on the kitchen table, Jim lit a cigarette and said to Veekay, "Calgary won't be so bad. You can escape in the summers. It's not like . . ."

Meg opened the ironing board and unrolled Jim's only white shirt.

"Like what?" Veekay asked.

She began to iron the back of the shirt, steam rising from the dampened cloth. She'd just have time to finish ironing and shower and change into her dress before they'd have to leave for the courthouse. Pray to God she'd be able to get the thin gauzy cotton buttoned over her breasts without tearing it.

"You're not sentenced to the tundra for life," Jim said. "Start applying for other jobs."

"It would be disloyal, seeking other jobs whilst tenure track at Calgary."

Jim guffawed. "That's the silliest thing I've ever heard."

～

Jim tossed his cigarette, half-smoked, onto the cold grate. June by now. "But you said you were on the Pill."

"I was."

"Then how could it happen?"

"I don't know," she wailed.

For two weeks they circled the problem, jackals gnawing on a carcass. Abortion. How? Where? There must be a way. He'd find out, give her the money.

She couldn't kill her baby. She couldn't.

And what about his plane reservation, the date fast approaching? She might go too. Where was the money going to come from? Her parents, maybe? Not hardly.

Let Jim go alone. Impossible, so long as this . . . *situation* . . . remains unresolved.

He bought the new Beatles album and, using earphones, plugged himself into his stereo and played the songs over and over. Across the room on the threadbare sofa, Meg watched the record going around and around on the turntable. She studied the titles of the songs on the back of the album cover. "Within You Without You." "A Day in the Life." "She's Leaving Home."

She thought, then, she was going to have to be the one to resolve the conundrum. She imagined herself moving somewhere distant and cheap like Maine, living in a little house by the sea, raising her child by herself.

Her mother and father drove to Cambridge for graduation. Holding her diploma, Meg smiled for the snapshots, the first in her family to have gone to college. Little did her parents dream there were two marchers under the rented black gown. Where's the father? they would have demanded to know. What's he going to do about it?

She admitted to her parents that she wasn't sure about her plans. Maybe she'd hang around here for a while, find a job, take a secretarial course in the evenings. Not surprisingly, her lack of direction exasperated them. Kevin all over again, they said, and look what happened to him. You don't have any idea what hard times are. All this expensive education, and you're sleepwalking. You have to grab opportunity when you have the chance. It may never come again.

The day after graduation, Jim telephoned the dorm. "Are you all right?" he asked.

She guessed what he meant was: Had she, by some stroke of luck, miscarried?

"Yes, I'm all right."

"I missed you, Meg."

She felt time pressing on her. "I have to move my stuff out of here," she said. "By the end of the week."

"Come see me. Please."

She walked to his place and they made despairing love in the hot, stuffy, dusty bedroom, where half-packed suitcases crammed the floor space. She wondered whether this was going to be the last time.

But the next day he cashed in his airline ticket, and they found the apartment on Farnum Street and moved in on the first of July.

〜

The three of them stood bunched together in the corridor outside the judge's chambers. Meg hardly dared breathe, lest buttons explode from the front of her dress. Jim also seemed stricken with some kind of paralysis, the license and blood test certificates damply rumpled in his hand. Finally Veekay tapped his knuckles on the paneled oak.

From within came a muffled voice, and Veekay led them in.

"We have an appointment to get married," Jim said, laughing nervously.

"Ah . . . Names, please?" inquired the judge.

"James Michael Mowbry."

"Evelyn Margaret Phillips."

The judge glanced at the documents that Jim handed over.

"I didn't know your name was Evelyn," Jim said to Meg.

"It's not something I tell everybody."

Veekay searched his trouser pockets for the ring. The judge rose from his desk, lifted a robe from a coatrack, and thrust his arms through the sleeves. Long ago the walls of his office had been painted a grim shade of green, and time had not improved it. Above a file cabinet some of the surface plaster had cracked off, leaving an unpainted area in the shape of some remote land-locked country such as Bulgaria.

... by the powers vested in me by the Commonwealth of Massachusetts ...

Over their heads a ceiling fan turned lazily, rustling the papers on the judge's desk. Within moments she and Jim found themselves walking down the worn steps of the courthouse, man and wife.

"Perhaps I should have taken my father's advice," Veekay mused, "and gone into the law."

∾

At the last minute Jim fell into a job teaching a section of Brit Lit in the summer school when the guy who was supposed to do it came down with mono. Meg found a job selling joss sticks, bead earrings, scented soap, and roughly carved Buddhas in a hole-in-the-wall shop near the Square. She acquired geraniums for the porch and a throw cover for the landlord's filthy couch, and to celebrate the glorious Fourth they grilled hot dogs on a hibachi that Jim bought on impulse when he was in a drugstore for cigarettes.

But his books stayed in their supermarket boxes, stacked on the floor of the living room, and she decided not to do anything about curtains for the apartment while things remained so unsettled. They had no lease. He paid the July rent and she the August. Jim spent his evenings grading papers, his earphones on. Sometimes they went to the movies, mostly for the air-conditioning, and saw *I Killed Rasputin, Don't Make Waves, The Graduate, The Ride to Hangman's Tree*. Meg felt the baby kick, a definite kick. In her excitement she put Jim's hand on her belly, but he claimed not to be able to detect any movement.

When they fought it was over trivialities: her long hairs clogging the bathtub drain or his spending seventy-five dollars on
books and records the same week he'd yelled at her for splurging
on carry-out Chinese. After lovemaking sticky with sweat, she'd
lie awake for hours, too agitated to sleep.

She kept waiting for some word from Jim about their future.
Jim, as far as she could tell, was expecting divine intervention.

One morning in the second week of August, Meg came to the
kitchen to start the coffee and found maggots squirming in
the garbage can amid melon rinds and corn husks. She sat at the
table and put her head in her arms. In the bedroom the alarm
went off, the shower ran, a heavy truck groaned in low gear out
on Farnum Street. Then Jim, edgily impatient for his first cigarette of the day, wanted to know what was the matter with her
and why wasn't the coffee percolating.

"The garbage," she said.

"What about it?"

"Take a look."

"Jesus."

"I can't bear it. Get rid of it. Now." She knew her voice was on
the verge of hysteria.

Rusty metal scraped against rusty metal as he wrenched the inner can from the outer one. He swore. The screen door banged
behind him, and his footsteps on the rickety stairs became fainter
as he descended. But the stench of the horrible wriggling garbage
lingered. She thought she hated Jim then, insofar as she knew
who Jim was well enough to hate that person.

Today she would not go to work but instead withdraw the
hundred and nineteen dollars in her savings account, take the
MTA to South Station, and buy a ticket to Maine, where it was
cool and dry and maggots did not spring gruesomely to life in
garbage during the night.

Jim came back and washed his hands at the sink. He pulled a chair away from the table and sat beside her. "I think we ought to get married," he said.

A kid shouted something in the street. Far away a telephone began to ring. Jim picked a stray hair off her tee shirt and dropped it onto the linoleum. The phone went on ringing, twenty or more times. Then it stopped. Meg said, "I would like to live in Maine someday."

"Maine?" he repeated vaguely.

When he came home from teaching his class Jim called the county courthouse and found out what they had to do to get a license, got in touch with Veekay and invited him to witness the tying of the knot.

∾

As the party was getting started, the next-door neighbor came out into her yard and took her washing off the line. She limped over to the fence and said to Meg, "What's the occasion?" The woman had sparse graying hair and dentures that seemed loose in her jaw.

On her side of the fence Meg said, "We got married today."

"I thought you were already married."

"No."

"Well, good luck to you," the woman said and carried her wash basket into the house.

A cousin of Veekay's, an undergraduate at Tech, had helped Jim string wires onto the porch and set up the stereo components there. Out of the speakers blared the Beatles, the Stones, Dylan, Simon and Garfunkel. A dozen grad students and four or five classmates of Meg's who were still in town milled around the yard, eating picnic food from paper plates under overgrown lilac bushes. Veekay delivered a floridly circuitous toast, which began with a discourse upon the four stages of life (celibate student, householder, meditative anchorite, and wandering ascetic), went on to extoll — or did it? — the fulfilling of worldly duties, and concluded with an encomium on the sanctity of matrimony. Champagne corks popped, beer caps flipped onto the lawn. "Good going, Jim," said Howard Somebody-or-Other, clapping him on the back. "Got yourself a gorgeous bride *and* outfoxed the Selective Service system, all in one swell foop."

Plastic glasses crackled underfoot. Somebody tied the ribbons from the champagne bottles in Meg's hair. The hem of her long dress dragged in freshly cut crabgrass. Joints were passed around. Fueled by Budweiser, Veekay's intense, bespectacled cousin made a pass at a shy math major from Meg's dorm. Overhead, Paul Mc-Cartney sang "Fixing a Hole" again. No matter how many times she heard the song, Meg couldn't figure out the words. Was the hole where the rain comes in a hole in the ceiling or a hole in the head?

Dusk fell and the midges began to bite. The party was thinning out. Suddenly Meg remembered the cake. She ran upstairs.

It sat on the counter looking like a victim of some natural disaster, which even shoppers in a salvage merchandise outlet would reject. The frosting had softened in the heat, and the top two layers listed to one side, tipping the groom to a forty-five-degree angle and pitching the poor drunken bride onto her face. Meg righted her. Down the hall the toilet flushed, and Jim came into the kitchen. "Want some cake?" she asked.

"Why not?"

She picked up a paring knife, cut a bite-sized square out of the top layer, and tucked it into his mouth. "Sweet," he said, taking the knife and cutting one for her. They licked each other's lips and tasted beer, vanilla, sugar, cigarettes, salt, grass . . .

∿

Ever after, Jim would tell people that he got married on the day Brian Epstein died. In fact, it was two days later, on the twenty-seventh, that Brian Epstein, age thirty-two, discoverer and manager of the Beatles, was found dead in his London apartment of an overdose of sleeping pills — but Jim said it so often he came to believe it himself.

III

1973

AN ITEM on the front page of the *Guardian* spoke of the photochemical air pollution tormenting Londoners, who were already suffering from a protracted August heat wave. Peter wondered whether photochemicals could be the source of the rash that had developed inside his collar and the wristbands of his shirt once he'd arrived at Paddington less than an hour ago. He exited the tube at Archway, crossed under the road in a urine-stinking and graffitied concrete tunnel, and emerged into late-afternoon light. No, you certainly couldn't call it sunshine. Buses idling at the various numbered stops contributed exhaust to the general miasma. Peter switched his briefcase from his right hand to his left and started up the hill.

As he climbed he felt a pulling sensation in his hamstrings — not enough exercise, too much sitting in a carrel. His wrists itched. Also, a sort of weight dragged on his heart that he attributed to low barometric pressure. He pictured the heaviness as a layer of stiff gray fat, such as you might find inside a fowl when you eviscerated it.

He passed an Indian restaurant, a dry-cleaning establishment, a pub, a newsagent. A young woman pushing a pram and endeavoring to manage a small dog headed toward him. The dog's lead kept becoming entangled with the pram's wheels, considerably impeding her progress. She had unrestrained reddish hair and a long cotton skirt which hung down as far as the pavement; the hem would be dirty, Peter thought. Her face was round as an apple, flushed with the heat, amused at her own hapless predicament. When she went by him their eyes met, for a second only, and a flicker of something like recognition seemed to pass between them. He returned her smile. From the woman's dress he imagined that she was a recent immigrant and might speak a foreign tongue.

After another five minutes' walk he reached Enid's flat, in a three-story brick building on a shaded side street. The tile-floored entryway was dim and a little musty. He ignored the elevator, which he'd found to be unreliable, and at the top of the stairs he felt winded. He knocked on her door. At first he thought she hadn't yet arrived — some important matter had detained her at work, after all — but then the door opened.

"Hello, Peter," she said. Her cheek was cool, and he fancied powder came off on his lips, as from a moth's wing. "I was surprised when you rang up, I must say."

He opened his briefcase, removing a bottle of Pouilly-Fuissé. "Perhaps you'd pop this in the fridge," he said. He thought she received a glimpse of an airmail envelope inside the briefcase, but if so she wouldn't inquire about the sender or the contents. She'd simply assume it was from some friend he'd made the year he spent on a postdoctoral fellowship in America, and in that supposition she'd be more or less right. "Did you have trouble leaving the office early?" he asked.

"Grovestein's on holiday in Wales. While the cat's away . . ."

But he knew Enid was far too responsible, and ambitious, to slack off only because her immediate superior wasn't on the premises. She'd be a partner in the firm someday, if she stayed.

"A cup of tea, Peter?" she asked.

For a moment he imagined himself turning and bolting through the door, running down the stairs, abandoning the expensive wine, never coming back. But the calm practicality of Enid's voice reassured him. He felt at ease in the order and graciousness of her flat: the polished old furniture she'd inherited from her parents, the faded Turkish carpets, the books arranged according to subject and author, the framed engravings of the Lakes on the wall. "Yes, please," he replied, and sat on the sofa. Taking the wine with her, she went to the other end of the flat. From the kitchen came familiar sounds of water coming to a boil, the clink of china being arranged on a tray.

When she returned, Enid sat across from him, in a chair with a floral print. She'd learned how Peter liked his tea: medium strong, enough milk to color it beige, one level spoonful of Demerara sugar. In a bit of a daze he watched her perform the ritual of preparing it. Her fingers were long and slender, the knuckles unusually prominent. Once, during a concert in the Albert Hall, when his eyes had strayed from the program they shared to the hand that held it, he'd wondered how, if somehow she managed to slip a ring past those knuckles, she'd ever get it off again.

"You said you wanted to talk to me about something, Peter."

In the hall outside he heard footsteps. Someone laughed, and a door at the far end of the hallway clicked open and then shut. He heard himself beginning to talk about his appointment at the college — secure, he'd been led to believe; the research project he was working on, which might well lead to publication as a monograph; the prospects — modestly bright — for further fellowships and grants; the friend whose uncle was a partner in a respected firm of solicitors there and would no doubt put in a good word if Enid were to . . .

Through all of this Enid sipped occasionally from her teacup, looking at him with a faintly bemused expression on her narrow face. He recalled his mother's assessment of Enid after their first meeting: *No beauty, surely, but good bone structure. In the long run that's more important in a woman; bone structure is what lasts.*

"I wonder," Peter said finally, "if you'd consider marrying me," and she set her cup on the table and replied that yes, she would consider the possibility.

～

Back in January, when the doctor affirmed her suspicion that she was, indeed, pregnant again, in spite of the diaphragm, in spite of liberal applications of spermicide, Meg had felt both wildly happy and sick with despair. She drove home to the messy old house in Wagasauken, New Jersey, and shut herself in the half-bath off the kitchen and sat on the toilet seat next to the cat box and wept.

For three months she'd left Peter's Christmas letter unanswered. When she did write she spoke of the burgeoning signs of spring in the yard and the return of the robins. She referred to the monograph Jim was working on, which would, he hoped, clinch his tenure bid. She mentioned her son Kevin's lovelorn fixation on his preschool teacher. No word about the child growing inside her. She expected, she didn't know why, that Peter would sense what was happening to her body, to her life, and find some way of letting her know how he felt about it.

But Peter's next letter, which arrived two weeks after she mailed hers, wrote only of the cool and rainy weather in Oxford, a concert he'd been to that featured Mahler's valedictory Ninth Symphony, a cold he'd contracted at the beginning of term which he hadn't been able to shake. He concluded with an amusing anecdote about going down to London to take his mother to the podiatrist.

As always, Meg put Peter's letter among Jim's mail on the table in the breakfast nook, and as always Jim left it unread. The moment Jim had abandoned medieval studies for the Renaissance, Peter's communications had ceased to interest him. Now and then, for no other reason than to hear Peter's name spoken out loud, she'd mention him to Jim, recall some event from the old friendship during graduate school days. Jim would mumble mm-hm, clearly thinking of something else. In some ways it was lucky that Jim was so oblivious. But what good did his denseness do her, after all?

Now, in August, she carried the morning newspaper out into the yard and carefully lowered herself into a canvas lawn chair. Under her sundress the baby lurched. A kicker, this one, much more active in the womb than Kevin. There'd been a few panicky times during her first pregnancy when the baby was so still Meg was sure he had died. No such fears about this one.

Kevin rode his bike the whole length of the driveway, the gravel spitting beneath the training wheels, back and forth, back and forth. Some kind of insect buzzed in the hedge, a lawn mower droned somewhere in the neighborhood. Forcing herself to stay awake, Meg unfolded the newspaper. The front page was entirely devoted to Watergate-related stories, even though the Senate hearings had gone into recess, with the exception of a piece about the U.S. bombing of Cambodia. Inside, on the foreign page, she saw a one-paragraph item about a package bomb that had been delivered to, and defused at, Number 10 Downing Street, the explosive concealed inside a hollowed-out book on Gustav Mahler. The prime minister, the article noted, was a devotee of Gustav Mahler.

Mahler. Meg imagined Peter picking up an envelope that lay among the mail in his Oxford apartment. The envelope would be slightly thicker and heavier than most letters and the postmark a foreign one, perhaps mailed in the United States. The address would be typed on a machine with a faded ribbon, the letters irregular, nervous, jagged. Oddly, the envelope gave off a faint scent of almond. A little puzzled or curious, possibly even hoping that the letter might be from her, he'd take his letter opener and slit the end and . . .

A cramp seized her belly. She let the newspaper drop onto the grass. Don't be ridiculous, she told herself, the IRA does not target Oxford dons, even those who go to Mahler concerts.

But the whole point of terror is that it's random, you never know when or where it might strike. And when it's not random, but executed according to some design, the terrorists are by definition rabid, people who make crazed connections and see conspiracies everywhere. Their targets could be anyone.

She fixed her eyes on Kevin in his red and white striped shirt and denim jeans, peddling his doggedly mundane course up and down the driveway. Maybe concentrating her psychic energies on the dull and innocent and ordinary would, by some form of magic, keep Peter safe.

～

He sat in his office at the college, a narrow and stuffy room crammed with books and journals and photocopies of vellum manuscripts. Before putting the airmail letter away for safekeeping, Peter read it one last time. Such simple and offhand words: *Another baby's on the way, due the end of this month.*

Stupid of him to be so surprised and disappointed. What had he been expecting, that one day she'd ring him up from Heathrow and say, "Here I am?"

As long as there was only the one child, the boy he'd once watched Meg nurse at her dining table amid the debris of half-eaten chocolate birthday cake and empty claret bottles, her coming to him must have been a possibility he'd kept somewhere in the recesses of his consciousness — even though he'd never framed the idea as such and would have been horrified at himself if he had dared to do so.

In her letters he'd detected, or imagined that he did, subtle intimations about her feelings for him and unspoken promises about a time, in the hazy future, when somehow Jim would not be a factor. He had not allowed himself to think about what she and Jim did in their bedroom. But this new baby, mentioned so casually, as if it were the most ordinary thing in the world for a married couple to produce a child — and of course it *was* — demonstrated the absurdity of his assumptions.

And yet even now, ten days after receiving Meg's letter and caught in the flurry surrounding his engagement to Enid, Peter could not quite believe that Meg would never be his.

Although he'd been seeing Enid on a regular basis since they'd been introduced by a cousin of hers, who was married to one of Peter's friends in the college, he had not mentioned her to Meg. There'd been no reason to. The relationship was a casual one: When he went down to London he'd ring Enid and perhaps take her to a concert or include her in whatever plans he'd made to amuse his mother. Enid had the desirable effect of defusing the one-on-one relationship with his mother, which could become uncomfortably intense. At times Peter wished that he were not an only child, that Mrs. Finesilver had more than one basket in which to place her eggs, so to speak, and to some extent Enid served that purpose. She was gracious and well-spoken, a success in her own right, far from the grimly needy and socially awkward spinster one so often encountered in the academic world. But marrying her had not entered his mind until this letter from Meg. The alacrity with which Enid and Mrs. Finesilver had sprung into action following his proposal suggested that marriage had, nevertheless, entered *their* minds. Ruefully Peter smiled.

He pulled from a top shelf a tin which had once contained wholemeal biscuits. Inside were all Meg's letters, perhaps two dozen in the five years since that memorable birthday party. He laid this letter on top of the others and returned the tin to its shelf. Through the casement window his glance fell on a patch of grass that had turned brown in the heat wave. A don hobbled across his line of vision, his gown flapping like the wings of a lame crow. Peter could not help seeing his future self in the old scholar, whose mental faculties as well as eyes had been clouded by a half-century of poring over manuscripts.

He returned to his desk and uncapped his fountain pen. *Dear Meg,* he wrote. *This may perhaps come as a surprise to you. I am engaged to be married. The young woman is named Enid Strudwick, and she is a lawyer in a large firm of solicitors . . .*

No, he could not bring himself to send such a letter, or even to complete it. He tore the page across, then again several times, and dropped the pieces into his wastebin.

∼

At two-thirty in the morning Meg awoke to the clutching ache in her belly mixed with nausea that suddenly she remembered from her first labor. How could she have forgotten? Her nightgown was soaked, and the cotton sheet felt unbearably heavy. In the bathroom she knelt in front of the toilet and tried to make herself vomit, but all that came up was a little acrid yellow fluid. Slowly the pain eased. Thinking she might faint, she moved away from the toilet and put her throbbing forehead down against the tile floor. How cool it felt.

She heard sounds in the hall. "Meg?" Jim called. And then suddenly he swore.

He stood in the bathroom doorway, his pale straight hair mussed, his blue eyes watering in harsh fluorescent light. "I stepped on a fucking . . ."

"A fucking what?"

"Hair ball."

She laughed, and then, reluctantly, he laughed too. He unrolled a length of toilet paper and wiped the dense woolly mess off the sole of his foot. "What are you doing on the floor?" he asked.

Another contraction had begun, this one harder than the last. "Baby's coming. Get dressed and wake Kevin up. Put a jacket over his pajamas."

Jim lifted the toilet seat and peed. "Why do they always choose the middle of the night?"

"To annoy you, Jim."

He flushed the toilet. "Meg, I wish . . ." But he didn't finish what he'd started to say, instead turned and left the bathroom.

When the contraction faded she shed her nightgown, leaving it where it lay, and washed her face and hands, brushed her teeth. In the mirror on the bathroom door she stared at her belly streaked with puckered ribbons of stretch marks, her splayed blue-veined breasts. Down the hall Kevin whimpered as his father roused him. "But I don't *want* . . ."

On the way to the hospital they left Kevin with Meg's friend Katie. Jim navigated the station wagon through a maze of empty dark streets, descending into fog as they reached the Wagasauken and crossed the bridge. The land near the river was swamp, covered with marsh grass and cattails, smelling of decaying vegetation. At this time of night you could imagine strange things in there: pet alligators grown huge, poisonous snakes thick as your arm with forked flickering tongues, covertly dumped chemicals or nuclear waste oozing into the muck.

Abruptly they emerged from the fog and were climbing the steep hill on which the hospital sat, its emergency room light burning all night. Neither spoke until Jim parked and turned off the engine. "Let's hope this one's a whole lot easier than Kevin," he said. "That was the roughest goddamn night of my life."

Only then did she think of Peter, how he'd come to the hospital the day after Kevin was born, shyly bearing a bouquet of tiny pink roses, politely avoiding notice of her haggard appearance. Jim, she remembered, had brought her a bunch of orange gladioli much too big for any of the hospital's vases.

∼

With the advent of September the weather turned dry and cool. One Sunday Peter took the train into London and he and Enid walked in the park near her flat. They talked about whether the wedding — now fixed, without Peter's quite knowing how, for a date in early April — should take place in London or Oxford. Peter described to her the college chapel, built in the seventeenth century, and mentioned some music that might be played during the ceremony: Bach's Organ Prelude in C, "Jesu, Joy of Man's Desiring."

"Your brother and his family are in Swindon," he pointed out. "That's closer to Oxford than to London."

"Yes," she acknowledged, "but I've lived in London ten years. My friends are here, not to mention my colleagues in the firm."

"Soon you'll be leaving the firm."

They stood on the edge of a pond, watching a child tear up slices of stale bread and hurl the bits at a clamoring raft of ducks. Enid took a moment to compose her reply. "Connections are important, Peter, in my sort of work. And what about your mother? Surely London would be more convenient for her."

True enough, his mother had begun to draw up a list of her friends to be invited. One couldn't expect all those dear old ladies, some with bad hips, to deal with the tube and the capriciousness of British Rail. In the end, Enid's quiet logic prevailed.

The following Sunday they met at Peter's mother's flat in Kensington. Peter carved the joint while Mrs. Finesilver served boiled sprouts, boiled potatoes, julienned parsnips and carrots onto each bone-china plate. Mint jelly shivered in a cut-glass bowl. The conversation between the women turned around the shockingly high cost of food and the rash of bombs in the Stock Exchange, Baker Street Station, even the West End. Nowhere was safe, they agreed. A person could open a perfectly innocent-looking letter and have a hand blown off, or worse.

Peter's thoughts drifted to Meg. No communication had come from her since early August, not even one of those printed cards that announce name, sex, and birth weight.

After the trifle Mrs. Finesilver took Enid into the sitting room and showed her the leather-bound album in which were mounted photographs of Peter as a child. Born just after Dunkirk, a puny infant. "He would have fit into a teacup," his mother said to Enid. The two women smiled, their smoothly coiffed heads bent over the album. On Enid's ring finger was his grandmother's emerald-cut diamond, which his mother had removed from a bank vault and given him to present to his fiancée.

∼

November rain forced its way between roof shingles, fell into the attic, eventually pooling over the bedroom, so that a stain and then a crack appeared in the ceiling, which began to ooze drips of dirty water. Jim called a roof man, who estimated that it would cost eleven hundred dollars to reshingle the house. Jim settled for a patch job. Meanwhile, the stain and crack remained. Meg stared at it as she sat propped up on the bed, nursing Michael. His mouth sucked hard at her sore nipple. He seemed to have an insatiable hunger, this child; her breasts couldn't keep up. But La Leche warned you not to supplement feedings with a bottle or your milk supply would decrease accordingly, a vicious circle.

Jim, just home from his daily six-mile run, yanked off his shirt and tossed it in the hamper. "I heard today the conference paper was accepted," he said.

"That's great." She unhitched Michael from her nipple and held him on her shoulder for burping. Gently she patted his back as he grabbed fistfuls of her hair. How silky his neck felt against her lips.

"I put in for travel money. The chair told me I'll probably get it, but he has to run it by the dean."

"Where's the conference?"

"London," Jim said, sitting on the edge of the bed to remove his shoes. She felt the mattress jounce under his weight. "February. Not the greatest time of year to be in London, but I'm not complaining." Jim's bony-shouldered back was to her. His running shoes thumped onto the floor.

London. She wondered if he'd make an effort to see Peter, maybe even take the train to Oxford. If only she could think of a plausible excuse for accompanying Jim on the trip. But not in February, not with a kid in kindergarten and a baby at breast. She settled Michael, now asleep, in his crib and went downstairs to start dinner. *Sesame Street* was on in the den. Overhead she heard the shower running and, outside, rain spilling off the clogged gutter and landing in fallen leaves.

〜

At the beginning of December, Peter found a pale blue airmail letter in his box in the vestibule. He carried it upstairs to his flat and laid it on the table in his sitting room. He wouldn't open it quite yet. He hung his jacket in the bedroom closet, washed his hands, went to the kitchen and plugged in the teakettle. A few minutes past five. It would be only noon in New Jersey. He imagined her seated at her kitchen table, perhaps nursing her baby. He saw again the full breast, flowing with milk, that he'd gazed upon at her birthday dinner. May 1968, Meg's twenty-second birthday. He shut his eyes and remembered the ramshackle back porch of the house on Farnum Street; her soft mouth tasting of chocolate and wine; her long, curling, honey-colored hair tangled in his fingers; the scent of lilacs drifting up from the otherwise squalid yard; the sweet, sad moan in her throat; the murmuring of her husband and the other guests still at table. After the increasingly desperate kiss she'd gone inside and he down the steps, and the next day he was on his way home to England.

The kettle whistled. He fixed his tea and carried the cup into the sitting room. Chilly, this room, and dark. Without turning on the electric fire in the grate he set the cup on the side table by his chair, lit the lamp, and opened her letter. *Dear Peter,* he read. *I apologize for taking so long to write. It seems that I hardly ever have a moment to myself these days, but that's the way it is with a new baby. His name is Michael, after Jim's dad, and he's now thirteen weeks old. Healthy and flourishing, eats like a little pig. Pale fuzz for hair, blue eyes like Jim's . . .*

She went on to talk about a conference paper on Webster that Jim had had accepted, the long and rainy fall, the lines at the gas pumps, a leak in the roof, Kevin's progress learning to read . . . She asked about his work, hoped it was going well. He searched for some special message between the lines, but found nothing. Perhaps there never had been one.

He picked up the telephone and dialed Enid's number. "I thought," he said when she answered, "I might come down on Saturday this week and stay overnight."

"At your mother's place, do you mean?"

"No."

She hesitated for a second and then said, "That would be fine, Peter."

～

Someone told Jim about a farm where you could cut your own tree, and on the Friday before Christmas he and Kevin set off in the station wagon with a saw Jim borrowed from a neighbor.

Meg, grateful for the peace, fixed herself a cup of instant coffee and sat in the breakfast nook with the morning paper. With any luck Mike would sleep for another half hour before demanding his late-afternoon feed.

More about the Watergate tapes, runaway double-digit inflation, the energy crisis. An article about the auto-buying public's switch to compacts and subcompacts with the subtitle *The Painful Adjustment to Thinking Small.*

She turned the page and saw a grainy photograph of a train wreck: a long-distance shot of overturned coaches and twisted tracks in a bleak wintry landscape. The short accompanying article read: *LONDON, DECEMBER 19 (AP) — Fourteen people died and at least 40 were injured, some critically, when an express commuter train left the tracks at Ealing. The train, packed with Christmas shoppers returning to Oxford from London, plowed into an embankment and overturned. Investigation into the cause of the crash continues.*

Peter's mother lived in London. He could have gone down to accompany her to the podiatrist or to do her Christmas shopping and taken that train back to Oxford. He could be in the hospital. He could be dying of grievous wounds.

Meg went to the telephone and dialed 0 and asked for the international operator. Eventually she reached Directory Enquiries in Oxford: a helpful man with an accent very like Peter's. Yes, he had a listing for a P. F. Finesilver. Certainly, he'd be delighted to give Meg the number.

She wrote it on the grocery pad by the phone but didn't ring it right away. She opened the refrigerator and took out a bottle of ale, uncapped it, and poured some into a glass. Outside the kitchen window dusk had fallen. Flakes of snow were drifting down over the dead and frozen lawn. Five in the afternoon here; it would be 10:00 P.M. in England.

The beer tasted bitter, and the cold gave her a sharp pain over her eyes. She poured most of it down the sink and then dialed the codes and Peter's number. She heard the clicks of international and local connections being made, ending in a shrill double ring. On and on it went, shrieking in an empty flat. She would never see him again.

And then the ringing stopped and, sleepily, he said, "Peter Finesilver here."

Meg could not make her voice work. Her throat was strangulated, her tongue paralyzed. It would be impossible to say, "I thought you were dead, but since you're not, we'll just carry on with our lives as before. Go back to sleep, Peter." Gently she put the receiver on the hook.

The station wagon pulled into the driveway, and Jim dragged the tree into the kitchen. The cats, who had been dozing under the table, tore out into the hall. Kevin danced in excitement. Needles and bits of straw and dried mud scattered on the linoleum. Upstairs in his crib, Michael began to cry.

∽

At Christmas dinner in Kensington they remarked on the frightful crash at Ealing. No, they knew no one among the killed or injured. How fortunate it was, however, that the accident had happened on a Wednesday and in a week during which Peter had remained in London.

In an attempt to press their wage claim the coal miners had refused to work overtime, and power cuts were commonplace. To deal with the energy crisis the prime minister, Mr. Heath, imposed a three-day workweek for the nation. Enid's firm would be affected. Rather a somber holiday this year, all in all. After dinner they turned on Mrs. Finesilver's color console to watch the queen's Christmas address to her subjects, and then Peter accompanied Enid to her flat.

He'd spent the previous three days here, sleeping with her in her single bed, absorbing the clovelike scent of her hand cream, lavender in the bedsheets, mothballs folded inside extra woolen blankets on the closet shelf. Clearly she'd been surprised, although not dismayed by the urgency of his physical passion. He'd noted a secretive little smile playing around her face during Midnight Mass, and again as they ate their Christmas pudding. Her complexion was unusually flushed. It's going to be all right, Peter thought. Not precisely what he'd imagined, perhaps, but good enough. As his mother said, Enid was suitable in every way to be the wife of an Oxford don, educated and articulate, and he supposed it would not hurt that she earned a solid income to supplement his comparatively paltry one. They'd be able to put away a comfortable nest egg before children came along.

∾

Meg watched Jim cram rolled-up socks, underwear, several folded shirts into the overnight bag he always took to conferences. He never checked a suitcase, insisted on traveling light. He didn't have the patience to wait for luggage, didn't trust the fools to get a suitcase onto the right plane in time for its departure or, once at his destination, off again before the plane left for Singapore or some other god-awful place. As a result, somewhat rumpled, he would give his paper wearing the same suit in which he'd traveled overnight to London. "Rumpled is how the Brits expect Yanks to look, anyway," Jim said. "Arrogant patronizing bastards." He'd exaggerate his Ohio twang to throw them off and then stun them into blithering incoherence with the depth of his scholarship, the nimbleness of his argument, the bite of his wit.

When he was nearly packed she asked, the words sounding falsely casual in her own ears, "Do you think you'll see Peter?"

Jim stepped over Kevin, who was playing with Legos on the

bedroom floor, and seized a tie from the rack. "Finesilver?" he said vaguely. "He won't be at this conference."

"I thought you might visit him in Oxford, or he could meet you in London for a meal or something."

Jim balled up the tie and jammed it into a side pocket. "I don't know, Meg. I doubt I'll have time."

"Look, Mom, I built an airplane," Kevin said. "Vroom."

"Good job, Kev," Meg said absently.

As the plane was making its maiden departure, from the lid of her sewing basket, the tail section fell off.

"You and Peter," she said to Jim, "used to be such close friends."

"That was then. Anyway, I don't know how close we were. Remember how he screwed me over the Digby Magdalen paper."

"What do you mean?"

"If he'd stirred his stumps and given me a little help with the damn thing, I might be tenure track somewhere decent right now instead of moldering at this third-rate excuse for a university."

"You didn't expect Peter to do your work for you, did you?"

"Whose side are you on?"

"I'm not on anybody's side. Look, if I give you his telephone number, will you think about calling him?"

"I'll think about it," he said, zipping up his bag. If it occurred to him to wonder why she possessed Peter's telephone number, he didn't ask.

~

After the Monday afternoon tutorial with his student Whipple, Peter decided to return to his flat rather than walk to the college library, as was his habit. Whipple had been even duller than usual, and himself shamefully short-tempered. He felt a little under the weather, perhaps coming down with a cold. Foolish to sit in the drafty carrel when he could work perfectly well at home.

He was brewing a pot of tea when the telephone in the sitting room began to ring. Odd, he thought, no one he knew would be likely to ring him at this hour. Some stranger must have misdialed. He left the pot to steep and went to answer it.

"It's Jim Mowbry," said the voice at the other end of the line. "Remember me?"

A wave of guilty chagrin passed over Peter, as if his thoughts about Jim's wife had somehow prompted the man to materialize, a disembodied spirit accidentally summoned from the ether. "How lovely to hear from you, Jim. Where are you?"

"I'm over for the R.S.R.S. conference, staying at the Brampton Hotel near Russell Square. I fly out tomorrow, but I thought you might be able to meet me for dinner here this evening."

Seeing Jim Mowbry was the last thing Peter felt like doing. He came very close to begging off — the press of work, another engagement. And yet from Jim he'd hear news of Meg. For the first time in nearly six years he'd be able to hear her name spoken aloud, even if the speaker was her pompous, brash, irritating husband. Peter looked at the clock on the mantel, calculated the time it would take him to travel from his flat to Russell Square. "I wouldn't be able to get there before seven at the earliest."

"Let's say seven-thirty, then. There's a Greek restaurant across from the hotel, do you happen to know it?"

"I'll find it," Peter said.

~

At 3:10 A.M. Meg picked up her fussy infant from his crib; he was teething already at six months, one incisor sprouted and worrying at a second. "Nyaa, nyaa," Michael complained, sucking furiously on her shoulder. She carried him to the wooden rocker by the window and unbuttoned the front of her nightgown. It had begun to snow in the night; along with the slurping sounds of Michael's nursing, she heard soft whishing against the glass.

Past eight in the morning in London, now, and within a few hours Jim would be on the plane heading home. What if there were a flaw in an engine, she thought, or the failure to tighten some crucial bolt? She imagined the tail section dropping off, the plane tumbling into the sea. She'd be a widow and, except for her children, free.

Hating herself for such thoughts, she began to weep. She hugged her baby against her breast and willed herself to pray to God for Jim's safe return.

~

In the morning Peter discovered the cold teapot full of swollen Earl Grey leaves that he'd abandoned the afternoon before in his hurry to catch the train to London. He dumped the tea into the sink and the leaves into the bin, rinsed out the pot, and plugged in the kettle. He'd slept badly, troubled with indigestion. Too much of that gritty, coarse wine, far more drink than he was used to. He regretted the moussaka. He regretted the whole evening. Why ever had he imagined Jim would say anything about Meg other than nebulous banalities: *Oh, you know, busy with the kids . . .* So self-centered as to be oblivious of his wife, and always had been. To no purpose had Peter ventured out into the chill February drizzle, and now he was paying for his mistake.

In the restaurant, irritated by Jim's monologue on the topic of his own situation and prospects, Peter had done something he'd promised himself on the train not to do: he'd disclosed his engagement to Enid. Yes, Jim had been taken aback. Peter knew the man deemed him an ineffectual permanent bachelor. Well, he'd proven Jim wrong, but the satisfaction had lasted no more than a moment. Now the news of his engagement would come to Meg secondhand, spoken in Jim's sardonic voice, perhaps on this very day.

If only that were all. Later on in the conversation, Jim had unexpectedly remarked on Peter's fondness for his wife. "Quite a few letters postmarked Oxford over the years," he'd needled. Jim's insight took Peter by surprise, even as his complacent amusement about it enraged Peter. He winced at the memory of his own words at dinner: "If you and Meg had chosen to part," he'd admitted, "I would not have been sorry." All those years of withholding his true feelings from Meg only to blurt them out, in a public place, to her husband. Peter detested having revealed himself so nakedly to Jim. No doubt this information would also get back to Meg. He pictured the two of them laughing over the hopeless delusions of a besotted medievalist. *Who would have thought? Poor old Peter.*

He could not face his usual egg this morning. He toasted two pieces of wheat bread on the grill above the cooker and ate them dry. Peter doubted that he'd ever felt more miserable in his life.

∾

Patiently Meg listened to Jim's account of the delivery of his paper and the responses it had elicited. London looked down-at-heels these days, he said. Dowdily dressed riders in the tube had pinched expressions on their faces, gripped their purse clasps like grim death. The Swinging Sixties were gone, all right, never to return. Meg did not ask Jim if he'd seen Peter. She figured he'd tell her about it if he had.

One day late in April, Meg sorted through the mail and came upon a small off-white envelope addressed in an unfamiliar hand and postmarked London. Inside was an engraved folded note announcing the marriage of Peter Francis Finesilver, Esquire, to Miss Enid Elspeth Strudwick on Saturday, the Sixth of April, 1974.

That afternoon she left Michael with her friend Katie and

drove downtown. After considerable deliberation she bought, in an antique store, a silver porringer. Late eighteenth century, the dealer assured her. He pointed out the hallmark stamped underneath. An elegant, if deceptively simple, little piece. One might use it to serve salted nuts in, or after-dinner mints.

Meg made Jim sign the card right next to her own signature so that Peter would not guess how much she was hurting.

IV

1986

THE CLIENT sat down and placed his briefcase beside him. Scuffed and buckled, it collapsed against the chair leg as if it were empty, or nearly so. He shed his parka and dug deep into a trouser pocket, producing a handkerchief with which he wiped his liberally freckled forehead. "A lot of steps," he observed.

"There's an elevator on the first floor, beyond the barbershop."

"I'd as soon walk up. Good for the heart."

"Right," Meg said, gathering her forces. She uncapped her pen and pulled toward her the basic questionnaire. "Let's start with your name."

"But I don't have one."

"You don't have a name?"

"Not yet." He looked at her expectantly.

Two months ago, when she began to work at Life Designs, Meg's boss had warned her about difficulties she'd be likely to encounter, such as clients who have in the past fudged on degrees and grade point averages and now present themselves with knotty inconsistencies in their supporting documents. Or those who enter your office convinced that their previous failure to land the job of their dreams can only be blamed on the existence of one evil reference, crouched like a scorpion somewhere in their confidential files, and who demand that you find the beast and exterminate it. Larry never mentioned this particular situation: a client who had no name. He made it clear, however, that he expected Meg to handle whatever crossed the threshold of her cubicle without running to him for help. "Out-of-work persons," Larry had said, "tend to be a little desperate, a little screwy. So be kind. But never forget, time is money. Don't let your client get out of control."

She decided to begin again. "What," she asked, smiling, "can I do for you today?"

The client stuffed the handkerchief back into his pocket. "I want you to design a life for me."

Patiently Meg explained that the name of the company was only a figure of speech. What they did was help clients shape and target goals, develop effective job-hunting strategies, market their skills more —

"You don't understand," he said. "It's not a question of fine-tuning a résumé. I need a new life story. From scratch."

Could this man have just been released from prison? Or from a mental institution? In spite of the awkward fit of his tweed jacket, he looked respectable enough — a reference librarian, perhaps, or a professor in one of the humanities, though she didn't recall ever seeing him at a university function. Clearly he didn't fall into a recognizable category of major misfits: He didn't have a week's stubble on his face and the aura of a goat, or weigh in excess of three hundred pounds, or fix wild eyes on the perforations in the ceiling tiles.

The client leaned over and unbuckled his briefcase, took out a lined yellow legal-sized pad. "So the first thing I need is a name," he said.

Meg laid her pen on the desk blotter. "What, exactly," she asked, "is wrong with the one you've got?"

The question seemed to puzzle him. "With the old name, I'd still be the old me."

"But you can't just reinvent yourself, as if the previous you never existed."

"I've already found that out." He crossed his legs, settling the yellow pad on his knee. "That's why I want you to do it for me."

He didn't seem obviously certifiable, yet Meg supposed there were people whose miswired mental circuitry became apparent only little by little. How best to get rid of this guy? She glanced at her watch: half past eleven. Perhaps, she thought, the thing to do was humor him until she could reasonably plead a lunch engagement. Then pray he never returned for a follow-up appointment.

"Well, let's see," Meg said, rolling her chair back from her desk a bit so she could take in the whole person. All his features were overlarge, almost clownish. Freckled hands as well as brow. No wedding ring. His thinning hair must once have been carroty, but had faded over time. Hazel eyes behind the kind of glasses that come two-for-the-price-of-one at chain eyeglass stores. A slight paunch under the wrinkled tweed jacket. Brown socks that seemed not quite to match. The names that fit his appearance — Walter, Norbert, Virgil — she couldn't in good conscience saddle him with.

She recalled the paperback baby-name book she'd bought when pregnant with Mike. The first name in the book was Aaron. She'd rather favored it on account of its ring of biblical rootedness, but her husband had dismissed the name out of hand.

"You look to me like an Aaron," she said.

Without protest the client wrote it down. "What about a last name?"

"Atkin." For some reason it had just popped into her head. Maybe she'd once known an Aaron Atkin, but if so, she couldn't remember where. Perhaps he was a movie director or a character in a novel.

"You seem pretty definite about that."

"Do you have a problem with Atkin?"

"Atkin will do very well." He wrote it down next to Aaron. "Where was I born?"

He didn't have an accent, not one that you could put your finger on, like Texas or Alabama or Maine. She guessed he hadn't fallen too far from the tree. "Newark."

"Newark," he mused.

"Your family lived in a three-room apartment above an oculist's office. You were the first child. A surprise to your mother. She'd planned on waiting awhile before starting a family."

In deliberate block letters Aaron was writing all this on the yellow pad. Meg rolled her chair closer to the window and looked down on Union Avenue, three flights below. In gusts of wind a paper bag scuttled along the sidewalk. "At birth you weighed less than three pounds," she continued. "Nobody thought you were going to survive, but you did."

Aaron made an odd little sound in his throat. Maybe he wished he hadn't.

"You were born during the war. Your father was on a destroyer somewhere in the Pacific and didn't hear about your arrival for months. Shortly after Japan surrendered, he returned home."

"I suppose my mother was glad to see him?"

The paper bag blew into the street and was instantly flattened by a delivery van. "As a matter of fact," Meg said, "she had mixed feelings. When she married him he was a happy-go-lucky kind of guy, loved to go out dancing and was always making wisecracks that would break her up. When he came home his jokes didn't seem funny anymore. She worried about money. He spent his spare time in bars with his old high-school friends or under the hood of the car making repairs. He lost his temper easily, at toys scattered on the carpet or when you cried at night."

"He never liked me very much, did he?"

"Mostly he ignored you."

"He must have wondered how he could have fathered such a clumsy son. Why no one else in the family had hair the color of mine."

Meg rolled her chair away from the window and picked up a stray paper clip from the desk. "Your mother wanted to move out of Newark because the neighborhood was going downhill. So they bought a little house in the suburbs, and soon your sister Ellen was born."

"Were we close, Ellen and I?"

"Not so much while you were growing up. But when you were teenagers, something happened to bring you together."

"What was that?" His pen was poised above the yellow legal pad.

"She got into trouble, and you found a way to help her out. She never forgot that."

He didn't ask what sort of trouble.

"She's long dead, of course."

"Oh," said Aaron, perhaps disappointed.

"Car accident, at the age of nineteen. You felt terrible because it was your car she was driving, and the brakes failed, and you thought by rights it should have been you that died."

Aaron recrossed his legs, rubbed his large nose. "It took me years to get over it."

"Yes," Meg agreed, prying open the paper clip. "Ellen wrote poems that won several awards, might someday have become famous. At the time she died you were studying to be an accountant. Accountants never become famous."

"An accountant? But I'm hopeless with numbers."

"You'd thought accounting, however tedious and numbing to the mind, would guarantee you a job. Death and taxes are always with us, and you preferred filling out tax forms to embalming corpses."

"I guess that makes sense."

"Employment security was important to you, of course, because of Anna."

"Anna?"

Meg looked at her watch and said, "I'm afraid I —"

"Would you allow me to buy you lunch?"

～

Meg didn't know why she was here, sitting at a table in the Dilly-Dally, across from this man with sparse once-red hair and fleshy ears and a lopsided, self-deprecating grin. It would have been easy to make up some excuse. She hadn't done it. He decided on a house special hamburg plate, cooked medium, and she the chicken salad. Without consulting Meg he ordered two Mexican beers.

As soon as the waitress had left he asked, "Who was Anna?"

"Hang on a minute, we're getting a little ahead of ourselves." She took a paper napkin from the dispenser in the middle of the table. "After high school you enrolled in college, here at Waga-sauken, when it was in the throes of transforming itself from a junior college into a university. Big new concrete high-rises were springing up all over campus. You had a partial tuition scholarship and a twenty-hour-a-week job shelving books in the college library. A Rotary scholarship covered books and other incidentals." She unfolded the paper napkin and placed it on her lap. "In your sophomore year you met someone, the ex-girlfriend of a guy who lived down the hall in your dorm."

"Anna?"

"Anna. English major. Brown eyes. Pearls in her pierced ears.

High arches. She gave off a scent you discovered to be that of aloe and almond soap."

"Ah," he said. His face flushed.

"Born and bred in southern California. To you, who'd never been west of Scranton, that sounded marvelously exotic, even when she mentioned that her town was inland, in desert country. You could hardly believe your luck in finding her." Meg paused. "It was not clear sailing, though."

"She did not return my feelings."

"No, she was very attracted to you, in spite of your —"

"Obvious physical deficits." His thick-fingered, freckled hand grasped his water glass.

"— doubts about yourself. Deep down, you feared Anna's love for you was flawed in some way, misguided. And she never knew quite where she stood with you. Sometimes she suspected she was merely a convenience."

"She was never a convenience. How could she have thought that? I was afraid to put my feelings into words."

"Because . . . ?"

"That might put the jinx on it. When the gods notice you're happy, they send down a well-aimed thunderbolt, or guide your footsteps over an open manhole."

The waitress brought two narrow dark-brown bottles, uncapped them, and poured the brew into glasses. Meg tasted hers. Yeasty, dense, a little sweet.

"Did we get married?" he asked.

With her napkin Meg removed creamy foam from her lips. "In your junior year," she said, "you switched your major to accounting. After graduating, you took a job here in town at a firm called Schatz and Schatz. Small potatoes outfit. Still, the salary was enough to get married on, and so in spite of some misgivings on both your parts, you did."

"What about the draft?"

"A heart murmur, perhaps the result of your premature birth, made you a 4-F. And, within a year of your marriage, Anna was pregnant."

"I have a child, then."

"Three daughters."

Their lunches arrived. He lifted the top of the bun and salted his burger. "Like King Lear," he said.

He had a literary bent, this accountant.

"Where are they now?" he asked.

As they ate Meg told Aaron about his daughters, the oldest one married and living on the West Coast, trying for a baby but no luck yet; the middle one a redhead like himself, a sophomore in college, prelaw; the youngest — named Ellen, after his sister — still at home with her mother.

Aaron set his half-eaten burger on the plate. "But not with me. I'm not there anymore."

"Well, no."

He nodded. They ate for a while in silence and then he said, "I still see my daughters, though. They haven't grown cold toward me."

"Oh, no. It's just the distance. . . of course, when children become adults they have their own lives, you have to expect that."

He finished his beer. Clots of foam clung to the inside of the glass.

"Will there be anything else?" the waitress asked, ready to slap the check onto the table. A small crowd of restless would-be diners milled around the door.

Aaron urged Meg to consider a dessert, butterscotch pudding or strawberry pie, at least some coffee. She had to get back to the office, she told him. One o'clock appointment, a ton of paperwork to do, jammed schedule all afternoon. Not the truth, but suddenly she felt worn out by his story.

"When can I see you again? How about tomorrow?"

"Tomorrow's pretty tight, too, most of the day."

"What about late in the afternoon?" he asked. "Say four-thirty?"

Tomorrow was Friday. She thought of telling him she was about to start a two-week vacation. Instead she said, "That ought to work out okay."

∾

Meg tuned the little transistor radio on the counter to catch the evening news and started to peel potatoes. . . . *reported today clandestine shipments of military equipment to Iran* . . . She pictured gun barrels, heavily lubricated firing mechanisms, crates of explosives swung by cranes into the holds of ships, under cover of darkness, on their way to a distant foreign country. . . . *the White House issued a blanket denial* . . .

The back door opened and shut and Jim came though the kitchen door rubbing his hands. "Can't find my gloves," he said. "Must have left them in the office or somewhere." His straight hair was awry, his cheeks reddened, his pale eyes watery from the raw November wind. "Smells like meat loaf again. What's the point in owning all those cookbooks if three nights out of the week you make meat loaf?"

"Isn't Mike with you?" Meg asked, switching off the radio. "You were supposed to pick him up from his appointment at the orthodontist, remember?"

"He'd left by the time I got there," Jim said.

"What time was that?"

Jim dropped his briefcase onto the table in the breakfast nook and got a bottle of Jim Beam out of the cabinet next to the refrigerator. He splashed some into a glass. "I don't know — around five-thirty, I guess."

"But his appointment was through at quarter to five. You said —"

"Just as I was leaving a student came charging in to whine over his midterm exam grade. Obnoxious sonofabitch, thinks all he needs to do is show up for the test and I'll give him an A out of gratitude." He gulped a swallow of the whiskey straight and then went to the sink and added water to the rest. "I think I'm coming down with something. Flu's going around, some nasty new Asian variety. My classes are half empty."

"Mike must have assumed you weren't coming and decided to walk."

"So? The walk won't kill him."

"But we agreed —"

"Mike's not a baby, Meg. He'll turn up." Jim lifted his briefcase and carried the glass of whiskey out of the kitchen with him. He hurried upstairs, the briefcase thumping against the balusters.

Meg shoved the peelings into the disposal and began to cut the potatoes into cubes. How many times, when Mike was little, they'd frantically searched an airport terminal, a zoo, a department store, when the kid took it into his head to wander. In despair she'd thought of roping a clothesline around his middle and tying the other end to her wrist. There might be laws against that, though. Bystanders would look at her with contempt. What does she think the child is, a dog? He could nurture the rope memory and carry it with him into adulthood, bring it to the attention of a whole succession of psychotherapists.

She put the cubes into a pot of water on the stove, lit the burner under it, and spooned 9-Lives tuna into a bowl for the cats.

For a while, Mike seemed to have grown out of wandering. But when he entered junior high in September, his unannounced disappearances started all over again. Last month the assistant principal called Meg at work to complain that her son had been regularly cutting his last two periods, gym and study hall. "What's going on?" she'd asked Mike. Those classes aren't important, he said. Why should he hang around the school when he could exercise and study more efficiently elsewhere?

The Saturday morning before Halloween Mike was supposedly at the church setting up for the annual autumn fair. "How's Mike's cold?" asked the chairlady next morning at church. "We missed him. He's always been so good with the streamers, nobody else dares climb that high."

"The old bat's confused," Mike said in reply to his mother's tentative question. "I unpacked must've been a hundred boxes of mothbally dresses and suits and hung them on those metal racks, the ones with wheels. No, I didn't tack up their dumb streamers this year. Why risk my neck?"

Meg might have found an offhand way to ask the elderly parishioner in charge of the Second Chance booth whether Mike had been one of her helpers. But what if she'd stared at Meg with perplexed, cataract-clouded eyes and said, "Michael Mowbry, the cute little boy who never knew the Bible verse in Sunday school? Oh no, I'm quite sure he wasn't in my booth." Which one of them would Meg have believed?

She turned down the fire under the potato pot.

One night last week Meg discovered Mike wasn't in his room doing his homework as she'd thought, wasn't anywhere in the house. "Naw," said his best friend when she phoned, "haven't seen him since algebra class." No answer in Jim's office — he'd popped over to the library to check on a reference, he explained later — so she got into the Saab and for over an hour drove through the downtown, and the campus and its outskirts, and around and around labyrinthine housing developments, some of which she hadn't even known existed. One fed into the other without notice or orienting signs or clear access to any road she recognized.

Then, on the point of pulling into a driveway and bursting into some stranger's house to alert the police, she suddenly found herself on familiar Glen Falls Drive. Right away she spotted Mike's pale hair illuminated by a streetlamp and recognized his sloping stride, so like Jim's. She braked and rolled her window down and yelled, "Goddammit, where *were* you?"

He stared at her as if she were an alien from space. "At this girl's house, working on a group history project. I told you."

"What girl? When did you tell me?"

"At breakfast."

She was sure he hadn't. Or almost sure. His face so bland — what did it hide?

At the counter, Meg sawed the tough end off a broccoli stalk. True, Kevin also had been closemouthed in early adolescence. But Mike's secretiveness seemed different from his brother's somehow, more ominous, in some way she couldn't specify. You hear about kids getting involved with drugs, with unsavory adults, with . . .

Upstairs the pipes rattled, Jim turning on the shower. Half past six by the electric clock over the refrigerator. It would have taken Mike no more than forty-five minutes to walk home from the orthodontist. She imagined him meeting someone in a back alley, struck by a car on the dark road, lying helpless in some ditch or field or patch of woods behind a stone wall. Thirteen isn't a baby, but in some ways it's even more hideously vulnerable. Perhaps, for a mother, the scariest age of all.

With a paring knife Meg divided the broccoli into thin, tree-shaped spears, finding each internally pitted as if by a boring insect or a deficit of nutrients at some point in the growing process. Upstairs the shower ran on and on, Jim relentlessly unconcerned about Mike's whereabouts. If there were a sudden telephone call, a need to go somewhere in a hurry, she would have to be the one

ELAINE FORD ~ 74

to do it. So although she'd have liked to take the edge off her nerves by pouring herself a glass of wine, she knew she'd better stay sober.

She opened the oven and looked at the meat loaf. Mud-colored, shrunken, surrounded in its glass baking dish by a sizzling moat of fat. Done, probably overdone, dried out, desiccated. Jim would leave the table and go to the refrigerator to extract the bottle of horseradish, spread it over each slice, eat the meat in martyred silence. She turned off the heat and left the door ajar.

Maybe, she thought, the problem with Mike was her own fault, the result of quitting her half-time job in alumni records and going to work in a real business downtown. Maybe he perceived the move as a kind of abandonment, especially since it had coincided with Kevin's departure for Antioch.

For an instant she thought about that clownish, middle-aged, sparse-haired client Aaron Atkin, whose materializing in her cubicle seemed even odder in retrospect that in actuality. Would he show up tomorrow afternoon? she wondered. Or had she, in some strange mind warp, invented the man — as well as his name and résumé — out of whole cloth? Yet she could almost taste the molassesy Mexican beer and feel its thick creamy head on her upper lip.

An out-of-control client, that was what Aaron Atkin was, the kind Larry had warned her of. What was the matter with her? How had she allowed herself to get drawn into his crazy project? Meg remembered Jim saying, more than once, that it's fine to encourage collegiality — professors and students equal partners in the search for truth and all that bullshit — but the minute a student starts to forget who's boss, that's when you lower the boom.

The water for the broccoli came to a boil, jittering the pot lid in a sputter of steam, and at the same moment the back door opened. With a swirl of fallen leaves Mike and two of the cats blew in.

"Where were —"

"Dad never showed up."

"You'd already left, Mike. It doesn't take two hours to —"

"I stopped off in the minimall and played a few games of Nintendo. Is that a crime or something?"

Meg dumped the broccoli into the roiling water and turned to look at him. Scrawny, pimply, teeth expensively wired, he was a shifty-eyed version of his father. She felt like slapping him for his wise mouth, for making her frantic with worry, for being so much like Jim. Instead she said mildly, "Dinner's in ten minutes. Go get washed."

∼

At quarter to five Meg looked down on darkening Union Avenue. In the lingerie shop across the street Christmas lights, which must have been strung up at some point during the day, winked on and off. To her surprise she felt a little let down that Aaron Atkin hadn't kept his four-thirty appointment. Maybe the whole affair had been some kind of practical joke or the payoff for losing a bet. She gathered the papers on her desk, filed a couple of photocopies. Drat, the Saab's in the shop, she remembered. She'd have to take a taxi home. And no one but the cats there to greet her, since Mike was going to the basketball game at the junior high school with friends and Jim to some academic meeting he couldn't get out of. "Bastards think they own you," he'd grumbled this morning over his bagel. "You might as well be in leg irons."

She pulled on her coat. As she was lifting the receiver to phone for a cab, she heard a knock on the door of her office. "I'm so sorry," Aaron said, panting. "Somehow the time got away from me." He must have run all the way up the three flights.

"It's okay, I —"

"Tell you what," he said in a rush. "Let's do this over a drink."

"Oh, I'm afraid that isn't possible."

A glove dropped out of his pocket, worn tan leather, lined with rabbit fur.

"No, of course not. Obviously, you have other plans."

"It's not that . . ."

The glove looked oddly forlorn, lying there on the carpeting.

"All right, let's," she said, amazed at herself. Larry would chew her out — maybe fire her — if he knew what she was doing.

Down on Union Avenue, Christmas lights were everywhere, not just in the lingerie shop. Their breaths puffed into the chill air. "Where shall we go?" he asked. "I don't know Wagasauken very well."

"Don't you? Schatz and Schatz was right down the street, in that office building across from the Dime Savings Bank. After you were married, and Anna was pregnant with her first baby, you and she lived in an apartment only a few blocks from here, over a used bookstore."

He smiled, as if that were a happy time in his memory. "But that was long ago, now."

"Things haven't changed very much, except for the mall out where the apple orchards used to be. Did you ever go there in the fall to pick your own?"

"No, I never got around to doing that."

"You'd have enjoyed it." She started walking toward the Ratskeller, which had good beer on tap and would be blessedly free of students. A scattering of snowflakes began to fall. A hard winter ahead, according to the *Farmer's Almanac*.

When they were settled in a booth and had ordered two dark ales, he said, "Tell me more about Anna."

It wasn't hard for Meg to picture her, the woman Aaron had

fallen in love with. "She had curly hair, dark blond — something like mine, except she always wore it short. A determined chin. You found her body enormously appealing, and assumed every other man felt the same way. When she told you she loved you, you didn't dare believe her."

The bartender brought their ales and placed them on little square cardboard coasters. With a freckled hand Aaron lifted his and took a deep drink. "I should have trusted her word," he said sorrowfully.

"There was one odd thing about her," Meg said, "which you didn't notice until you'd been married several years."

"What was that?"

"She'd rarely look straight at the person she was talking to. Her gaze would be elsewhere."

This early, the Ratskeller had almost no customers. Across the room the bartender stood alone, polishing glasses. Here Christmas lights had been hung, too, tiny unblinking white ones over the bar mirror and looped from rafters.

"What finally caused the rupture?"

"The reasons," Meg said, "were complicated, as I suppose these things always are." She took a sip of her ale. "By the time your third daughter, Ellen, was born, you were living in a small house over on Willow Road, having a tough time making ends meet. Old Mr. Schatz died, and you and the younger Schatz didn't get along very well. It became clear that you had little future with the company. You looked for better-paying work elsewhere in Wagasauken, without any luck. Then you found a job in a much bigger firm of accountants — Brace, Brace, and Colpritt — in lower Manhattan. The family left Wagasauken and moved to a house with twice as many rooms, in a town northeast of here, from which you could commute. In that house swirled a confusion of diapers, dental appointments, ballet lessons, hamsters, gerbils,

Barbie dolls, curlers on the sink, long hairs in the drain, menstrual pads, telephone calls from boyfriends . . . All of these bemused you and, increasingly, you felt left out.

"When Ellen started junior high, Anna joined a health club and took some pounds off. In partnership with one of her friends she opened an interior decorating business, which was successful right off the bat. More often than not you'd come home after the long bus commute and find no one in the house, only a scrawled note fixed to the refrigerator by a happy-face magnet. 'Leftovers in fridge,' the note would say."

Aaron nodded in recognition. He emptied his glass and motioned to the bartender for a refill.

"You never relished your job, that goes without saying, but now numbers began to blur before your eyes, even though you went to an optometrist and got a stronger prescription in your glasses. You'd make foolish errors. In the afternoons drowsiness would come over you so powerfully that you'd shut the door of your office and put your head down among the papers on your desk. One day your supervisor came in with some documents for you to work on and found you dead to the world. He gave you a warning. A month later it happened again and you received a second, more serious warning."

The bartender brought Aaron's ale and replaced the cardboard coaster, which had soaked through with sweat from the glass. He also brought a small bowl of salted peanuts.

"You found you could hardly deal with the figures at all anymore, so you had to fake your work. Numbers seemed like a language you once could speak but had somehow forgotten or a code you couldn't crack. Sooner or later, you knew, you'd be found out and fired. You thought you might be going insane or be suffering from some kind of dementia, so you made an appointment to see a doctor on your firm's list of approved health providers. But you didn't keep it."

Aaron licked foam from his lips. "Because I didn't want to know the truth."

"Because you didn't want to know the truth," Meg agreed. "Nor did you want to know what Anna might really be doing in those evenings when you came home to a dark and silent house."

He took a peanut out of the bowl and rolled it between his fingers. "And then what happened?"

"On a Saturday morning a man you'd never seen before came up onto the porch and rang the bell. When you went to the door, he thrust a sheaf of divorce papers into your hand."

"Was I surprised?"

"You hadn't seen it coming, but at the same time you weren't surprised. You moved into a small apartment in a nearby town. Your oldest daughter was already married by then and the middle one away in college, but you continued to see Ellen occasionally, when she wasn't too busy with her other activities. Somehow you hung on to your job, without knowing quite how."

"Did I grieve over the loss of my wife?"

Meg paused, her fingers touching the rim of her glass. "Your grief took the form of numbness. A person seeing you from the outside would not have known anything had happened to you. Even Anna had no idea how you felt, because you couldn't explain. You did not contest the divorce.

"At last the day came," Meg continued, "when, as you'd long been expecting, your supervisor called you into his office to inform you that your services would no longer be required. He didn't say whether the cause was a mountain of accumulated small errors or one final disastrous botch. You didn't ask. You might have left your office then, since there was nothing to pack into your briefcase except for a framed photo of Anna and the girls taken the year you went to work at Brace, Brace, and Colpritt. Out of habit, however, you lingered until the usual departure time.

"On the homeward commute the bus came to a dead stop in the tunnel underneath the river. You thought you heard a siren. The hefty black woman sitting next to you screamed and grabbed the handles of her shopping bag. Suddenly the aisle was crowded with passengers, jostling each other, pushing off the bus. In the confused jumble of sounds you made out a word: *Fire.* Fire somewhere in the tunnel. You smelled the smoke and knew it was true. Acrid fumes burned in your eyes, in your throat. Outside, the commuters ran past, among and around the stopped vehicles. Your bus was empty."

"Except for me."

"Yes."

"I figured I might as well die on that bus as anywhere."

Meg pictured Aaron seated alone, looking out the window into roiling yellowish smoke weirdly illuminated by a light on the tunnel wall.

"After a while," she said, "you got up from your seat and moved forward in the deserted bus, slowly, using little oxygen. You stepped down onto the wet, gritty pavement in the tunnel and began to walk toward New Jersey.

"You took a handkerchief from your trouser pocket and covered your nose. Your eyes stung and your heart felt as if wrapped in rubber bands, those tough tight ones that come around bunches of broccoli, and you had to breathe shallowly so that your heart wouldn't pain you too much.

"Water on the floor of the tunnel soaked through the soles of your shoes. The smell of metallic, chemical burning was sickening. You tasted salt in your mouth. Except for your own footsteps, the tunnel had by now become eerily silent.

"You realized you'd left your briefcase behind on the overhead rack, but you didn't go back for it. A glove fell from your coat pocket and you left it lying there on the pavement.

"The walk went on and on. It occurred to you that perhaps the fumes had killed you as you sat on the bus, after all. This journey was your hell or limbo or purgatory. You would never get to the end, or there was no end.

"Step by step you kept going, though. Eventually you made it to safety."

"Why didn't I stay on the bus?"

She looked at him. His face no longer seemed comical or strange to her. She felt as though she'd known him her whole life, and even before, in some other life. His hazel eyes held hers.

"Because," Meg said, "you knew there was more to the story."

Meg declined a meal, but rather than telephoning for a cab and waiting for it in the doorway of the Ratskeller, accepted Aaron's offer of a ride home. In the dark of Hawthorn Street they sat in his rusty Pontiac and he asked, "Do you have time for me on Monday?"

"I don't think so, Aaron."

"Tuesday, then."

So much she wanted to reach for him, gently kiss his cheek and neck and mouth, feel him stroke her face with freckled, thick-fingered hands. But who was he? A man completely invented. "No," she said. "I'm sorry."

A few dry specks of snow skittered on the windshield. "It would mean a lot to me."

"I've already told you everything I know."

"There's more to the story, you said so yourself."

"Yes, but you have to be the one to discover it." She opened the car door. "Good-bye, Aaron Atkin."

Meg cut across the crunchy lawn, blanched with the sparse snowfall of the winter, walked around the side of the house, and let herself in the back way. She found Mike in the breakfast nook eating a sandwich. Vaguely she wondered why he was home this early. Perhaps more time had elapsed than she'd thought.

"How did the game come out?" she asked.

He grinned, peanut butter stuck to his silvery braces. "We murdered 'em."

V

1991

"WHAT about this one?"
"Spindly," his father said. "When I was a boy back in Dayton, my dad would buy two trees Christmas Eve, the last miserable ones in the lot, knocked down to a couple dollars apiece. He'd saw the branches off one, bore holes in the other, and fit the branches into the gaps. He always said nobody would know the difference. *I* knew the difference."

Kevin had heard this story so many times it ranked right up there with the other apocryphal tales of the season: shepherds keeping watch in the fields, three wise men following a star. He wished he'd bothered to find a warmer coat instead of throwing on his denim jacket in the hope that the project would be over before the chill seeped through. More fervently, he wished he'd been as quick as Mike to come up with an excuse to bypass the annual tree-farm expedition altogether.

His father limped on ahead of him. He'd hurt his foot running, he said, twisted it under him. For some reason it was slow to mend. In Kevin's opinion his father would be better off giving the fitness kick a rest, but out of long experience he kept his mouth shut. Even when Kevin won an argument — winning constituted hanging in there until his father lost patience and threw his napkin onto the dinner table — it wasn't worth the struggle.

Kevin followed Jim over hillocks and swampy places thinly crusted with snow. In the distance gulls circled over a dump that was sending an aroma of burning tires into the ecosphere. "There," Jim said finally. "The perfect tree."

To Kevin's eyes it didn't look any better than the other one. Thicker trunk, though. Frozen, it would probably cut like iron, be a pain to hump over desolate acres back to the car. Kevin knelt in the snow and began sawing.

∼

The year after college, Kevin had interned in a Jersey congressman's local office. The guy was vaguely liberal, at least on environmental issues, and Kevin had figured the job would help him make connections, land him a position that would allow him to make a difference in people's lives. He'd spent the year trying to soothe enraged constituents who'd burst into the office bent on wringing the congressman's neck, only to learn their man was in D.C., doubtless being wined and dined by lobbyists and throwing away taxpayers' money.

Kevin drifted down to Texas, where one of his friends from a peace activist organization was living, and ended up working construction. He acquired a tan and firmed up his muscles, but no way was he going to crawl around on beams the rest of his life. He took the Greyhound to Boston, moved in with his college girlfriend, and found work in a soup kitchen. A couple of weeks ago he'd put in an application for a relief job in El Salvador and started learning Spanish from tapes.

El Salvador might be poor and war-torn, Kevin thought, fiddling with the wagon's heater knob, but at least it would be warm. "Is this thing busted, or what?"

"Needs a new resistor. Your mother never remembers to tell them when she takes the car in for servicing." Jim pulled off the highway into a strip mall, parked in the fire lane, and got out. "Just be a minute," he said.

The tree in the back of the wagon, now that it had thawed some, smelled distinctly like cat piss. Kevin watched his dad limp over to a video store and disappear inside. Next to the video store was a Radio Shack, and next to that a tee shirt emporium. Two days before Christmas, but already an after-Christmas pall hung over the place — big SALE signs in the windows, the tinsel garlands coming untacked. A guy with a cigar in his mouth was scattering salt onto the ice in front of the tee shirt store.

Jim returned with a video in a plastic bag. "What did you get?" Kevin asked.

"*The Graduate.*"

"*The Graduate?* That's on cable all the time."

"Not necessarily when I feel like seeing it."

"Plastics," Kevin muttered.

Jim jerked the wagon back onto the highway. "Why do you need to be such a smart aleck?"

Everything on the landscape seemed shut down for the winter. Frozen cattail stalks poked dismally out of a marsh. Kevin thought about El Salvador, where the temperature was probably in the high seventies, at least. "*¿Qué pasa, señorita?*" he said to himself.

~

Jim dropped him off at the house with the tree and left for the campus to do some busywork in his office. Instead of wrestling the tree inside by himself, Kevin leaned it against the house and went in the back way. He found his mother at the table in the breakfast nook, icing ginger cookies in the shape of Santas and elves. "Did you get a nice tree?" she asked.

"Yeah. Big fat trunk, though. I don't even know if it's going to fit in the stand. Where's Mike?"

"He said he had some shopping to do."

At the sink Kevin scrubbed pitch from his hands. "He took the Honda?"

"I guess so. I didn't hear him leave."

Snuck out, the creep. Won't be back until nightfall, if then. Kevin stepped over one of the cats, Mull, who lay curled on the linoleum, and walked to the table. He watched Meg dip a brush into a teacup of red frosting and paint a cap on one of the Santas. "I've always wanted to know," he said, "how come your Santas are hunchbacked."

She gazed at the cookies she was decorating as if she'd never thought about their shape before. "Those are packs on their backs. Full of toys."

Shoving some magazines aside, he sat on the bench across from her. "They look like hunchbacks to me." He helped himself to a green elf and bit off a leg. As usual, Meg had been generous with the ginger, and the peppery taste made him feel like sneezing. "Dad's got quite a limp," he said.

She pushed tendrils of hair back from her forehead. Her eyes looked tired, Kevin thought. Some gray in her hair now, too. "He turned it, running."

"He told me."

"Don't you believe him?"

"Sure I believe him. Why shouldn't I?"

"I don't know, Kevin. Something's wrong with his right hand, too. Sometimes he has trouble holding a pen, and he drops things."

"Has he seen a doctor?"

"He won't go. Says it's stress, that's all."

Kevin finished off the cookie, wondering what his father had to be stressed about. Tenured professor, nothing to do but spoon-feed *Midsummer Night's Dream* into kids a couple times a week, attend committee meetings now and then. Summers off, long vacations . . . a cushy life. Not that Kevin would be able to stand it himself, being trapped at a third-rate institution, nothing to look forward to but retirement.

Meg got up from the table and began to wash mixing bowls in the sink, aluminum grating against enamel. It occurred to Kevin that the kitchen looked different in some way. He couldn't put his finger on what had changed, though. Same catsup stains on the worn checked oilcloth, same old Kenmore appliances, harvest gold or whatever they called that color. Same faded café curtains, the speckled linoleum that always looked dirty even if Meg had mopped it, dishes grubby with rejected cat food by the back door. Yet he could swear something was missing, or out of place.

"How's Sharon?" Meg asked from the sink.

"Okay. She went to New Hampshire for Christmas."

"I thought her folks live in Kansas."

"She went skiing with some friends."

Meg set a bowl upside down in the drainer. "You could have invited her here."

"Here?" he asked stupidly.

"Are we so awful?"

"Sharon and I don't have that kind of a relationship."

"I assumed," she said, hanging the dishrag on a rack next to the sink, "when you got back together with her . . ."

"No, Mom, you don't understand. She was looking for somebody to help with the rent, and I needed a place to stay. We're friends, and that's it. As a matter of fact," he went on, "I'm thinking of going to Central America."

To his surprise, Meg looked stricken. "Whatever for?"

"To work for a relief agency. They told me I had a pretty good chance of being accepted, but I haven't heard definitely yet."

"But what if . . ."

"What if what?"

He thought she was going to say: *What if war breaks out? What if there's a revolution? What if you get thrown into jail on some trumped-up charge?* Instead she said, "It's so far away. Supposing it turns out your father is really sick, or . . ."

"Or?"

She turned away from him, to the counter. Her curly light hair had escaped its scarf, and corkscrews trailed down her back. "Have you told your dad?"

"He'd say, what do you want to do that for? Goddamn bleeding heart, exactly like your mother."

"Yes," Meg agreed. "He would say that."

∾

Before dinner on Christmas Eve Kevin took a can of beer from the refrigerator and went into the den. He'd been going to turn on the TV, but instead sat thinking about how strange it was that the house he'd spent nearly his whole life in didn't feel like home anymore. In a way he was almost a guest, his mother careful to consult him about menus and food preferences. Rather than going into his room and gathering the dirty clothes, she'd inquire whether he had anything to contribute to the washing machine. Jim, on the other hand, treated him more like an intruder than a guest. Sometimes his father would display annoyance but more often apparent bafflement over what, precisely, Kevin was doing here.

Kevin wondered whether Mike, back from his first semester of college, experienced these sensations, too. But Mike lived in his own little world, spacey even as a kid, always wandering off and getting lost in zoos and airports and museums. He probably wouldn't notice any change more subtle than the house having been leveled by a bomb.

Kevin had drunk most of the can of beer when he heard his father's uneven footsteps in the hallway. He expected the light to go
on and Jim to say, "What are you doing sitting in here in the
dark?" But Jim went to the telephone on the side table and began
rapidly to plink buttons on the receiver. After ten seconds or so,
he said softly, "Come on, Annie, I know you're there. Pick up,
dammit." Brief silence. Then, in falsetto, "*Leave a message at the
beep and I'll get back to you.* When's that going to be? When hell
freezes over?"

Jesus, Kevin thought, the jig's up now. But his father never saw
him. He slammed the receiver into the cradle and left the room,
and next Kevin heard his tread — a definite limp now — on the
stairs.

Beer surged up into his craw, and he forced it down again. He
remembered being pinned on the mat by a tough townie kid
when he was on the freshman wrestling team in high school and
afterward vomiting onto the locker room floor, a humiliation
worse than the public one that preceded it.

What was the matter with him? People had affairs all the time,
even people his father's age. It didn't mean that life came to an
end, or even that marriages came to an end.

Suddenly he wanted to talk to Sharon, but he'd never be able to
come up with the name of the ski resort where those guys had
sublet somebody's time-share. How was he to know he'd need to
reach her?

He sat on the sofa in front of the TV, light-headed on a can of
beer, and imagined various parts of his father's body shriveling
and falling off. His right hand, his forearm up to the elbow. His
foot, then his leg. His cock.

It had to be eighty degrees in this room, the thermostat turned
way up, the furnace going full blast. The rich, meaty smell of
whatever Meg was cooking made his stomach roil. He wanted out

of here, out into the cold night air. But he was the dutiful elder son, and if Mike didn't show up for dinner, not an unlikely possibility, that would be both of Meg's sons abandoning her on Christmas Eve. The tree still had to be brought in and set up and hung with ornaments. Kevin moaned and dragged himself off the sofa.

~

Chicken for Christmas dinner, instead of the obligatory bone-dry fourteen-pound turkey, and served at midafternoon, when they'd recovered enough from a late breakfast to have some appetite. Only one dessert — a store-bought mince pie with a cardboard crust. "I didn't want leftovers," Meg explained. "I promised myself I wasn't going to be stuck with leftovers this year." They shoved the bones into the trash and the dishes into the dishwasher. Mike took off in the Honda. Meg went upstairs, to do some sewing, she said. With a glass of port Jim took over the den to watch *The Graduate*.

The temperature had risen into the forties during the day, and fog drifted up from the diminishing crust of snow. Taking care not to clip one of the cats, Kevin backed the wagon out of the driveway. Dusk already upon him. He'd thought that like Mike he'd seek out some old friend from high school, but as he left Hawthorn Street and followed the curving stone wall along Glen Falls Drive, he realized that no one he knew was likely still to be around, or if they were, he wouldn't really want to hear their tales of botched opportunities.

After driving around in town, and out on the strip, and through a couple of mazelike developments strung with Christmas lights, Kevin found himself on the north end of the Wagasauken campus, near the steam plant. With the intent of reversing direction, he drove into a short, dead-end street next to the graduate student housing complex, and suddenly he had a recognition of having been here before.

Years ago — he must have been around seven or eight — his father had picked him up after his swimming lesson and then, instead of driving him straight home, said he had an errand to run. He had parked the car in this little dead-end street — Kevin was certain it was the same one — and then the two of them went past one or more gray concrete high-rises, into a building, up several floors in an elevator.

Kevin hadn't thought about her in all this time, but now he remembered her perfectly. Pale skin, odd-colored reddish hair combed close to her head. An actual tree grew in her apartment, seven feet tall, at least. He'd never seen a tree in a house before, except at Christmas. "What kind of a tree is that?" he wondered. "I think it's a kind of fig," she told him, and his father laughed. No fruit hung from the tree's slender limbs.

Strange smells in her apartment. Food, maybe, but not food like his mother ever cooked. He asked to use the bathroom and saw in the toilet bowl a small brown turd that hadn't flushed. For some reason his pee wouldn't let go. He washed his hands without soap and dried them on his pants instead of using one of her towels.

She made a great fuss over him, brought out a plate loaded with cookies, and when she leaned over to put the plate on the coffee table, her jersey sagged open at the neck and for a second he saw her bra. He didn't feel hungry, but ate a cookie to be polite.

Somehow he knew without being told that this visit was a private matter between him and his father, not something to be spoken of, so he didn't mention the detour to his mother. And then he forgot it, until this moment.

Kevin backed out of the street and drove home. In the den *The*

Graduate had reached the big climactic scene in which Dustin
Hoffman makes off with Katharine Ross in her wedding dress.
His father was asleep on the sofa.

~

In her ears Meg wore the diamond studs Jim had given her for
Christmas. They didn't suit her at all, in Kevin's opinion, hard
and glinty. So that the earrings could be seen she'd pulled her hair
back into a tight knot, which revealed her jawline in an unflatter-
ing way. New Year's Day she'd come down with a cold, and as she
drove toward the campus she kept pulling a ragged tissue out of
her pocket to blot her nose.

A hundred times between Christmas and New Year's he'd
started to say: *Dad's messing around with some woman, Mom. And
it's not the first time, either. Take those ridiculous diamonds, or zir-
cons, or whatever they are out of your ears and throw them in his
face.*

Each time his more sensible side had argued: *Why hurt her for
no reason? Sounds like the deal with this broad's over, anyhow. Keep
out of it, buster, it's no business of yours.*

He'd talked his mother out of driving all the way to Newark
Airport, mostly because he was weary of the quarreling voices in
his head and feared that in spite of his better judgment he'd spill
it all out. No, he insisted, he'd take the Campus Motel minibus. It
wouldn't cost much more than paying the turnpike tolls.

At the motel Meg pulled into a spot in front of the office and
turned off the ignition. Under the accordion-shaped metal canopy
a guy with a suitcase stood reading the *Times*.

"I hate good-byes," Meg said.

The lunch bag she had packed for him sat on Kevin's lap, emit-
ting a strong gingery smell. "Looks like it could snow," he said.

"You should get off the ground all right."

"What's the temperature, around freezing?"

"Around." They watched the guy under the canopy unfold his newspaper, turn the page, and refold it. "You and your dad didn't have much to say to each other."

Kevin shrugged.

As if coming to a decision, she stuffed her tissue into her pocket. "Kevin, I'm going to tell you something."

Uh-oh, he thought. Where the hell is the bus?

"When my brother got killed I'd just started my senior year in college."

Her brother? What's he got to do with anything?

"For various reasons," she went on, "Kev's death really hit me hard. I stopped going to classes and eating proper meals. I figured there was no point in learning anything or staying healthy if you were going to walk into a land mine and be blown to bits. Or some other totally unfair thing was going to happen to you. So why bother, you know?" She pulled out the tissue again and snuffled into it. By now it was in shreds. "Or maybe you don't know."

"I read you."

"I was pretty much of a mess, barely scraped through the fall term. In the middle of the night I'd wake up and ponder various ways of putting an end to my misery. But I didn't know where I'd get a gun, or how to fire a gun even if I had one, and I had no access to sleeping pills or any drug like that, and a razor or a knife seemed so awful, all that blood, after the way Kevin died, and —"

"Mom."

"I felt even worse about myself then. Not only a coward, but incompetent."

A light rain began to mist the windshield. The guy under the canopy looked at his watch. No sign of the minibus.

"Anyway, in the spring semester one of my courses was Chaucer, and your dad happened to be my section man. He asked me to come to his office to talk about a bad grade I got on a test. He was so nice to me, I blurted out everything about Kev, and the stupid way he died, and how hopeless I felt. Your dad said, 'Let's go get some coffee,' and I guess so people on campus wouldn't see my tears, he took me to a place in town. We sat at a little round table, and drank Turkish coffee in tiny cups, and he bought me a pastry made of almonds and honey. It was wonderful." She paused, as if she were tasting again the sticky, overly sweet cake. "I'll never forget how kind he was that day."

Again the other passenger looked at his watch. If the minibus didn't come soon, Kevin was going to miss his plane. The rain would turn to sleet and ice up the wings of every plane Continental owned. He'd be hanging around that godforsaken terminal waiting for the weather to clear until the end of time.

Feeling doomed, he clutched the neck of his lunch bag. "That was then, Mom. Now is now."

"What I'm trying to tell you is, don't be quick to judge, Kevin. Things are never quite the way they seem."

What *was* she saying? The hunchback is deep down a Santa? Or the Santa turned out to be a hunchback?

"Mom —"

Around the corner of the motel tootled a dirty white minibus. The guy shoved his newspaper under his arm and climbed onboard with his suitcase.

"You better go." She leaned across the seat to kiss Kevin's cheek. "Call when you get to Boston. Promise?"

"Promise." He got out of the car, grabbed his duffel from the rear, and hurried to board the bus before it left him behind.

VI

1992

WITH HER long-handled squeegee Orla reached to the top of the plate glass, beneath the cracked, furled awning. Years — possibly decades — of grime loosened, combined with soapy water, and coursed down the window in depressing black rivulets. She plunged the squeegee into the metal bucket and yanked the lever back to wring it out, let the sponge soak up more water, tried again. But the liquid in the bucket had become so filthy that the glass muddied over worse than before. Sweat formed in Orla's armpits.

She leaned the squeegee against the building and dumped the swill into the gutter. Dirty water sloshed onto her bare legs. Somebody, she noticed, was standing in the street watching her. He was maybe an inch taller than her own five-ten, pale straight hair, acne pitting the corner of his mouth, backpack slung over his shoulder, a mostly eaten apple in his hand. She figured he'd been observing her at work while finishing his lunch — about all this town had to offer in the way of entertainment. He took a bite of the apple and said, "Messy job." Without replying, Orla lifted the bucket and started inside.

For some reason he ambled along behind her, past show-cases displaying gold-filled lockets, birthstone rings, silver baby cups. Orla's father, attending to the innards of a watch, did not look up. In the back of the store Orla went in the primitive, partitioned-off utility room, and the guy followed. "You work here?" he asked, dropping his core into the wastebasket under the sink.

"Sort of." In fact, Orla was only helping her father out in odd hours, while looking for a short-term job that actually paid. In the fall she'd be going away to college in Indiana.

"Allow me." He rolled up the sleeves of his striped shirt and took the bucket and ran water into it almost to the top. He poured in some Spic and Span, twice as much as she'd have used, and carried the bucket back down the narrow aisle, spilling only a little on the cranberry-colored carpet. Outside, he set the bucket down on the sidewalk.

"Thanks," she said.

After a moment he took a second apple out of his backpack. "Want one?"

The fruit was of a size that you buy individually, for at least a dollar a pound, not the puny kind sealed in plastic bags. "I don't think so."

"Well, see you," he said, and walked away. For a moment she watched him go, a little annoyed with herself for having declined the gift.

∽

When she'd finished the windows, Orla rearranged the entire case of Keepsake wedding and engagement rings. Around four o'clock, irritated at her fussing, her father said, "Your mother could probably use some help in the kitchen." But Orla was not ready to return home yet. She got in her car, a dilapidated 1983

Chevy that her brother Danny had abandoned when he went in the service, and drove it down to the far end of the street. A sprinkle now dappled the sidewalk in front of Snooky's Luncheonette, with promise of more serious rain to come.

Orla went inside, ordered coffee at the counter, and carried it to a scratched Formica-topped table. In Snooky's, lighting was provided by fluorescent tubes attached to the ceiling. Wall decorations consisted of warnings from the management that the Board of Health required shirts and shoes to be worn and that a microwave operated on the premises, which, if you had a pacemaker, might cause your heart to stop. Dreary Snooky's certainly was, but currently Orla was into dreary. In the library some months ago she'd come upon a reproduction of a painting by Edward Hopper. *Nighthawks,* it was called. The people in the picture knew things, mysterious and fascinating and soul-wrenching things. Snooky's was the closest thing to Hopper around here.

She'd drunk her coffee about down to the dregs when he came wandering in, the guy in the striped shirt. Surprise: She'd assumed he'd be long gone down the expressway by now. At first he didn't see her. He stood at the counter and studied the menu board, ordered a grilled cheese sandwich. Then, holding the tray, he turned around. "It's you," he said.

Orla returned his glance but didn't say anything. She knew she looked more composed than she felt. When she was eleven she'd sprung up like a newly rooted willow branch and found herself faced with a narrow choice: stoop to be part of a jocular crowd or remain gravely aloof. Because she couldn't pull off the former, she'd done the latter. Once somebody said that her smooth dark hair would be neat even in a windstorm. It wasn't, she suspected, meant to be a compliment.

He dropped his backpack onto a nearby chair, settling himself at her table with his plate of grilled cheese, ribbed potato chips, and slice of dill pickle. He was on his way home from college in Ohio, he told her. If it took a while to get there, well, he felt in no special hurry. The driver of the pickup who gave him a ride this afternoon could have taken him as far as Harrisburg, but when he saw the sign for the town of Utley he decided to take a small detour. Something about the name roused his curiosity, the solidly straightforward but at the same time vaguely comical sound of it. Like a bank president with buck teeth. Or a college professor with hemorrhoids. Right?

Orla smiled.

What he likes is the unexpected. The revelations you can find only in out-of-the-way places. Serendipity. Meeting an interesting person engaged in washing a small-town jeweler's windows, for instance.

Orla smiled.

He'd finished his sandwich and was working on the last of his chips. The pickle slice remained on the plate. It's not the destination that's important, it's the journey, as his old man was fond of saying. Now, though, he had to hit the road.

"I'm going in the direction of the turnpike," she said, the words tumbling out of her mouth, "I'll give you a lift."

He reached over to the chair at the next table and picked up his backpack.

~

The rain was coming down harder now. They hurried into her car, and he flung the backpack onto the rear seat. Orla switched on her wipers to maximum speed, then her headlights.

He had a nice smell, she thought, like clothes when you've brought them in off the line. At the foot of Elm Street they crossed a stone bridge and at the fork headed out Larch Road, which quickly left behind the newly built split-levels and capes and wound through wooded countryside. Lightning crackled. He asked her name and told her his: Michael Mowbry. Mike. Suddenly thunder boomed behind them, and he laughed.

He's not at all like Utley boys, Orla thought, whose heads you have to gaze over when you're dancing with them. Who are destined to pump gas or to work at some store out at the mall unloading crates marked THIS END UP — and have trouble figuring out which end *is* up.

Too soon, signs for I-76 appeared. She came to a stop on the side of the road a few feet before the on ramp. "You'll be drenched," she said.

"It doesn't matter."

"Why don't I give you a ride up to the next exit? Maybe the rain will stop by the time we get there."

Orla pulled onto the on ramp and they took off down the highway, heading east. Traffic sparse, free sailing. He began to tell her about a movie he'd recently seen on campus, an old Italian film called *La Strada,* about circus performers on the road. It wasn't the plot that grabbed you, he said, but the characters. When they reached the next exit he was still talking about the movie and rain continued to spatter the windshield, so she didn't stop — or at the following exit, either.

"Sure you want to do this?" Mike asked. "You're going pretty far out of your way."

Back in Utley was her house with its cramped rooms that smelled of dog hair and cheap cuts of meat boiled to gray stringiness. Dreary all right, but not *Nighthawks* dreary. Boring dreary. In her future was a small Catholic college in Indiana that nobody ever heard of, that her parents had chosen for her.

Why, come to think of it, should she be in any hurry to get to either place? "I'm sure," she said.

Before long Mike's hand lay on her shoulder, lightly fingering the material of her blouse, and he was telling her about his dad, a professor of English and expert in Renaissance drama, and his mother, who wrote résumés for people, concocting new lives for them.

∼

Somewhere east of Harrisburg they decided to stop for something to eat, and Orla took the next exit. The town was on the confluence of two rivers hardly bigger than streams, with a couple of gas stations, some closed stores, and a warehouse or two. Nobody on the street, darkness gathering. For food, the choices seemed to be a pizza place opposite the railroad tracks and, a bit farther on, next to a motel, a Chinese restaurant called Heavenly Delight. They decided on Chinese.

The woman who ushered them to a booth was hardly Chinese, and the menus she gave them bore the evidence of years of chop suey. Mike ordered a couple of beers, and nobody asked to see their IDs, and after a few sips Orla felt gloriously happy. "You realize," she said, "I have on me seven dollars and change."

He waved his hand. "I've got nearly forty dollars, plus plastic."

"And I have to call home and let them know I haven't been left for dead in a ditch."

"Will they be upset?"

Will they? Through a beery haze Orla considered the question. "I guess I'll find out," she said, picking up her purse and heading for the pay phone near the john.

Her middle sister answered the phone. "Where the heck are you?" Mary Pat said. "You missed supper."

"Tell everybody not to worry, I'm fine. I'll be home in a few days."

"A few days! Mom'll bust a gut."

"She'll get used to it."

"No way. It'll be just like when Danny joined the navy."

"I'm not joining the Navy, Mary Pat. Just say I'll be back soon."

"Maybe they'll think you've been kidnapped," Mike said upon her return.

Orla finished her egg roll and wiped her mouth with her paper napkin. "Nobody in their right mind would kidnap me," she said. "No money for ransom."

∼

After dinner they gave the motel next door the once-over. From the outside it wasn't too intimidating: a one-story strip of adjoined rooms, twelve or fifteen of them, each with its own window air conditioner whooshing strenuously into the humid June air. "I wouldn't . . . you know," Mike said. "But we could use a good night's sleep, especially you." He went inside the office, leaving Orla behind the wheel, and soon came back with a key.

Inside their room it was like Guatemala, or what she imagined the climate of Guatemala to be. Mike fiddled for a while with the temperature control knobs, which he discovered secreted under a panel on the radiator, before their air-conditioning agreed to kick in. The double bed was covered in ragged fringed chenille with cigarette holes burned into it; on the wall hung a painting of the Grand Canyon at sunset. Suddenly the traveler in the next room turned on his shower, and their own plumbing rattled as though about to explode into hundreds of lead projectiles.

Mike sat on the edge of the bed and removed his sneakers. His dropped socks, collapsed on the tacked-down rectangle of carpet next to the bed, looked to Orla like roadkill. "Which side?" he asked.

"What?"

"Which side of the bed do you want?"

"The outside, please."

He offered her the use of the toothbrush he extracted from his backpack, which she politely declined. Within ten minutes he was dead to the world.

∽

At 4:20 A.M. a giant truck, which had somehow parked itself near their room — how could Orla have failed to hear it arrive, lying awake the whole night? — started up its engine, rumbled awhile, and finally roared out of the lot. Half-light. She returned her wristwatch to the nightstand and listened to the hum of the air-conditioning. Under the bedspread Mike snorted and turned over, dragging the spread with him. Orla did not know the name of the town she was in, was not even sure whether it was still Pennsylvania. Maybe she should get into her shorts and drive quietly out of the lot, back to the highway, taking the route west. He'd be a bit surprised to find her gone but would have no trouble hitching a ride out to the turnpike. By noon he would have forgotten her.

In his sleep he turned toward her, his knuckles against her thigh, his face near her upper arm. She felt the moisture of his breath on her skin, through her blouse. For a long time she lay absolutely still, hardly daring to breathe herself lest she waken him, because she liked these feelings. He shifted again, perhaps dreaming, and his body moved closer to hers. More time passed, she had no idea how much. But his breath dampened the nape of her neck now, and she guessed, but did not know for certain, that he was not asleep anymore. She felt a solid nudge against her buttocks, and then his fingers slid inside the elastic of her underpants and gently touched her between her legs.

He got up and switched on the light. "Do you want me to go on?" The acne pit in the corner of his mouth looked deeper now. His straight pale hair fell across his brow.

She didn't say anything.

He found his wallet somewhere in the clutter on the dresser and took out a flattened packet. It looked as though it had been secreted there some time, like a cough drop in a twist of waxed paper that you come upon in an old coat, years after you put it there.

She turned toward the wall and heard him rip apart the wrapper, felt him crawl back under the cover. Right away he grasped her, his hands on her hipbone and her crotch, and bucked until he got inside her. It hurt so bad she thought he must be doing something wrong and tried to wrench away, but then he shuddered, crying out, his cheek pressed flat against her spine.

∽

"You didn't do it before," he said.

Somebody walked across the gravel right outside the motel room.

"No."

"You could have told me. You're not deaf and dumb, I'm not a barbarian."

She didn't reply, didn't know what to say.

He spent six of his remaining twenty-eight dollars on breakfast in the diner by the railroad tracks: scrambled eggs, sausage links, hotcakes, hash browns. In the booth he flipped though the juke-box selections, most of them country and western, but made no move to deposit a quarter. He still wore the striped shirt, now much the worse for wear. "Do you want to go home?" he asked.

"No."

"It would be okay. Just leave me near the on ramp heading east."

She shook her head.

They went back to the motel room, since he'd kept the key and they weren't required to check out until eleven, and he used the remaining two packets in his wallet.

∼

"When I was a kid I got lost all the time," Mike said.

Late afternoon, and by now they'd picked up the Jersey Turnpike and were heading north. When they left the motel the second time he'd changed his striped shirt for a plain blue one, which was full of wrinkles, but clean, at least. Orla still wore the blouse she'd slept in. She had no idea where they were heading except that it was in New Jersey somewhere, and she began to worry about what would happen when they got there. Maybe he'd say "thanks for the ride," and lift his backpack out of the rear seat, and that would be that. On the other hand, if he took her inside, what were his parents going to think about the way she looked and how she happened to land in their laps? Maybe this wasn't such a great idea.

"In airports, the science museum, shopping malls," he continued. "It gave my parents fits."

"How did it happen?"

"They claimed I wasn't paying attention. It seemed obvious to me that they were the ones not paying attention."

"I'm famous," Orla said, "for having a good sense of direction."

"Really?"

"In the family. I do the navigating whenever we go somewhere." Which wasn't too often, as a family, because it was nearly impossible to round up all eight of them at once and squeeze them into her father's station wagon, but she didn't say that.

"A useful skill," he said.

"But you probably know the way from here."

"All you have to do is follow the signs."

After a while she said, "What if the signs are confusing? What if they don't take you where you intended to go after all?"

He laughed. "Then you make a U-turn and start over."

∼

A few minutes past seven they pulled up in front of a big white Victorian on Hawthorn Street in the town of Wagasauken. Now he's going to say it, she thought — so long, nice knowing you — but he grabbed his backpack by a strap, opened his door, then stood on the strip of grass bordering the sidewalk, waiting for her to fold her sunglasses and set them on the dash. They walked around to the rear of the house, past an iris bed and up some steps, through a screen door into a little entryway, where jackets and sweaters hung doubled up on pegs and underneath, all higgledy-piggledy, were six or seven pairs of running shoes in various stages of wear. Inside the kitchen he called, "Hey, it's me."

His mother came rushing in and ran to hug him. She was half a foot shorter than Orla, with graying fly-about hair and dark eyes. "We weren't expecting you so soon," she said, giving Orla a warm smile in spite of the calflike long bare legs and rumpled blouse.

Mike explained that he got a ride practically door to door, and this is Orla, and maybe she could have Kevin's room since he's in El Salvador. "I thought we'd be right in time for dinner," he said, looking around the kitchen as though expecting to see a standing rib roast materialize on a platter. The only signs of food preparation were some pots drying in the drainer.

"We've fallen into the habit of eating early these days," his mother said, "but I'll reheat the lasagna. There's lots." She lit the oven and took a shallow glass casserole from the refrigerator.

"Where's Dad?"

"He's upstairs. Mike," she said, when he started to leave the kitchen, "wait a minute. We need to talk before you go up there."

Oh geez, Orla thought, what have I stumbled into? "Maybe I'd better —"

"Why?" Mike asked. "What's wrong?"

His mother slid the casserole into the oven and pushed her curly hair back from her forehead. "We didn't want to put this in a letter. We thought we'd wait until —"

"You're getting a divorce. That's it, isn't it? I thought something was out of whack at Christmas, the way Kevin kept scowling and the two of you were walking on eggs."

His mother flushed. "We're not getting a divorce." She put her hand on Orla's arm and said, "Let's sit down."

"I really think I'd better be . . ." But Mrs. Mowbry was directing her firmly toward the breakfast nook, where there was a table with a catsup bottle and a paper napkin holder in the shape of a garden cart on the faded oilcloth. Orla sat on one of the benches, Mike beside her. He or his brother must have made the napkin holder in shop class, Orla guessed.

His mother went to the refrigerator and took out three cans of beer, then sat across from them. "Or maybe you'd rather have a Coke?" she said to Orla.

"No, this is fine." Her second beer in two days, when before that she couldn't have had half a dozen in her whole life.

"What's the story?" Mike asked.

"Remember the way your dad was limping at Christmastime?"

"Yeah, he twisted his ankle running."

"Remember how I made Kevin carve the chicken?"

"You said Kevin ought to practice for when he had a family of his own, which was pretty tactless, come to think of it, since he and Sharon hadn't exactly seen eye to eye on the question of marriage, and Kevin was about to leave for El Salvador, probably as a way to evade the whole ball of wax. He certainly made a hash out of that poor chicken."

"Mike, listen to me. Your dad's sick."

"What do you mean, sick? Like the flu?"

"No, not the flu. He has a serious disease. A fatal disease."

A gray tabby jumped into her lap, and absently she stroked it while telling them about amyotrophic lateral sclerosis, and how it affects the neurons in the brain, and gradually a person's muscles waste away until he can no longer button his own buttons, or walk, or talk, or swallow.

"Jesus, he's not —"

"No, not yet. In fact the doctor says he's doing well, considering, and he plans to go on teaching, one more year, at least. But early in the spring he fell down a flight of steps on campus and broke his leg. He still doesn't get around easily. He's lost weight, quite a bit of weight. So I had to prepare you, before you saw him."

"How long does he have?"

"Maybe three years, if we're lucky. Maybe less."

"No cure?"

"No."

Mike turned his beer can around and around and around. Then he got up and went out the back way, letting the screen door bang behind him.

"Mrs. Mowbry," Orla said, "I really apologize for blundering into this. If I'd known, I —"

"No, it's good you came, you'll be a distraction. And do call me Meg."

She served Orla some hot lasagna and then, when Orla confessed that she had no luggage with her, not even a toothbrush, Meg fixed her up with some clothes Kevin had left behind in his closet and bureau. "Tall and thin," she said, "like my boys. Your hair, though. Nobody in the family has lovely dark hair like that."

∾

At dawn Mike came into Kevin's room and stripped out of his clothes and slid into the single bed next to Orla.

"Did you just get back?" she whispered.

"Walked all over town."

In the dim reddish light she could see the shapes of model airplanes hanging on threads from the ceiling.

"I went to his girlfriends' old places," Mike said. "The graduate housing by the steam plant. The apartment over the orthodontist's office downtown. The condo in what used to be the armory. The row house on Irving Avenue."

In spite of herself Orla was shocked. Though her parents had waged small-scale warfare ever since she could remember, her mother in shrill chain-smoking complaint, her father in tight-mouthed silences that might last weeks, Orla was sure neither of them had ever slept with anyone else. Their lives were too frazzled and pinched for either of them to manage an affair, even if they'd wanted one.

"While I was having my teeth straightened my father was upstairs fucking this scrawny graduate student. Can you believe that?"

"How did you know where they lived?" she asked.

"For years I tracked him and his girlfriends. For the sport of it."

Birds, sounded like robins, were beginning to chirp in a tree outside Kevin's window. In some air current that Orla couldn't feel, the model planes rocked a little.

"Did your mother know?"

"If she did, she hid it well."

"You didn't think of telling her?"

He was quiet for a while. Then he said, "It was strange. I despised my father for what he was doing. I thought he was a jerk for being so clumsy I could catch him at it. Still and all, I could see his side. Not the screwing around with students, that's totally sordid, but the adventure."

Mike wound his arms around her. After a while she felt damp-

ness on her back, his tears soaking into his brother's baggy tee
shirt. "He's a son of a bitch, all right," Mike said. "But I don't want
him to die."

ᴀ

Orla had eaten a bowl of cold cereal and was now at the sink
washing the few dishes that remained from Meg's breakfast and
her own. Meg was off to work, Mike still sleeping. On the sill behind the sink stood a row of bottles holding cuttings of various
houseplants, several in each container. Most of the cuttings had
grown elaborate root systems, which were now intertwined in
murky water. Mike's mother must be one of those people who
can't throw away so much as a twig, as long as it's alive. Orla wondered how Meg would get the clumped roots out of the narrow-
necked bottles without damaging the roots or breaking the glass
when she went to transplant them.

She heard limping footsteps on the hall stairs now. Mike's father. "You must be the girl Mike brought home with him," he said
from the doorway. "I didn't catch the name."

"Orla."

"I'm Jim," he said, heading unsteadily for the coffeepot on the
stove.

"Can I get you anything?"

"I'm not a cripple . . . yet." He took a mug from the row of
hooks above the stove and poured coffee into it. "You at college
with Mike?" he asked.

"No. I met him in my hometown."

"Where's that?"

"Utley, Pennsylvania."

"What in the name of God was Mike doing in Utley, Pennsylvania?"

His tone of voice annoyed her, even though she'd be the first to
call the town dull. "Just passing through."

Jim laughed. "Sounds like him." He carried his mug to the table in the breakfast nook. Orla wished she could escape. However, he'd begun to talk about his own forays into darkest Pennsylvania: how he was once lost in some obscure neck of the woods and in a foggy, weirdly lit landscape saw a bunch of cows huddled against a barn. For a strange, disorienting moment he'd felt himself bodily transported to England. "Anything like that ever happen to you?" he asked.

No, she confessed, nothing exactly like that. Her back to the counter, Orla watched him pour milk from a carton on the table into his coffee and stir it. The man was much like his son, except that the pit in the corner of his mouth was a dry scar, his hair thinning, his face ruddy. Yes, Orla could see that he'd lost weight. His shoulders seemed to be caving inward toward a shrunken chest; when he lifted his mug his steel expansion watchband slid loosely on his wrist.

"Come keep me company," Jim said, and since she couldn't think of any excuse not to, she sat on the bench opposite him. "Plan on staying here long?" he asked.

She met his eyes, which were light blue and watery, the whites slightly bloodshot. The hand holding the mug trembled slightly. She sensed in him a restless energy, barely contained, that helped her to understand why all those women wanted to sleep with him, and yet he repelled her, too. Maybe it was the thought of the disease eating away at his muscles.

She had no intention of telling him that for the first time in her life no plan was laid out for her, not even for the next ten minutes. Instead she said, "Not very long," but he didn't seem to have heard her answer anyway; he was launching into another story, this one about a time he actually had been in England, roaming the Wessex countryside during the hottest summer ever recorded there, and stopped for lunch at a pub where he imprudently ate cottage pie that had been languishing too long on the sideboard, and ended up sick as a dog.

"That was before Mike was born, of course. That was before Mike was even imagined."

~

In the late afternoon Orla lay in the grass reading a detective novel she'd found in Kevin's bookcase. Up on the roof Mike hammered nails into shingles. His father had, with effort, clambered halfway up the ladder in order to monitor Mike's progress. Soon Meg came out to the backyard with a paper sack and a colander, opened up a lawn chair next to where Orla was lying, and said, "He wouldn't listen to me if I told him he's going to fall and break his neck, so I might as well save my breath."

"Mike?"

"My husband. I'm sure Mike would be happy enough to be called down off that roof." Meg sat and dumped some peas into her lap. With her thumbnail she slit one open, and *plink, plink, plink* went a row into the colander. "I bought these at a farm stand on my way home. Nothing tastier than fresh peas, don't you agree?"

"I hate the frozen kind."

"Until last summer I grew peas myself." She glanced at an abandoned garden patch, where some shriveled, rotten cabbages crouched among weeds. "But that maple has gotten so big it hogs most of the sunlight, and I've kind of lost heart for vegetable gardening. What did you do today, besides watch Mike hammer nails?"

"He showed me around a little. We walked on the campus, ate lunch, drove through the downtown."

"Where'd you eat?"

"It was called Sally's, I think."

"Ah, yes, Sally's. Sally was one of Jim's graduate students, long ago."

Orla reached into the bag for a handful of peas and, sitting cross-legged on the grass, began to shell them into the colander. "That's what Mike said."

"For some reason she stayed around after she graduated. Couldn't find a job in English, naturally, so she opened that little café."

"No, not there," Jim yelled from the ladder.

"This is where the shingles are loose," Mike yelled back.

"That's not where the leak is."

"The water could be traveling a ways before it finds a spot to break through."

"Bullshit. Do it the way I tell you to, dammit."

"She used to be a very attractive young woman," Meg continued, ignoring the altercation on the roof. "Bright, too. It's a pity she'd grown so attached to the town she didn't want to leave when she had the chance. That window of opportunity can be incredibly small, people don't realize. Then it slams shut."

Plink, plink, plink, plink.

"It's best not to get too attached to places. Or things, either. Of course" — Meg grinned — "that's advice I haven't taken myself."

A shaggy cat with brown, white, and orange splotches emerged from the barberry hedge and crossed the lawn, rounded the corner of the house and disappeared.

"I haven't seen Sally in years," Meg went on. "For some reason I don't find the time to eat out much."

She should make some reply, Orla thought, but it would sound so dumb to say something like, "Tell me about your job." She brushed an ant from her leg and reached into the bag for more peas.

"How's the food at Sally's these days?" Meg asked.

Orla guessed she had better be careful with her answers. Maybe Meg was trying to find out how much Orla knew about seamy family history. "It's okay," she answered noncommittally. "I had a burger stuffed with blue cheese. Mike had Belgian waffles."

"I wish I could eat a burger stuffed with blue cheese," Meg said, smiling, "and be as thin as you."

A hammer went sliding down the pitched roof, bounced off the gutter inches away from the ladder, and landed in the iris bed. Jim's bellow could probably be heard all over the neighborhood. "What's the matter with you? Are you trying to kill me?"

Meg sighed, gathering the empty pea pods into the bag, and picked up the colander. Under the ladder she said to Jim, "Come on down before you kill yourself."

To Orla's surprise he did what she asked, painfully slowly, rung by rung. Together the two of them walked to the back steps and into the house.

∽

The next day Mike took Orla to the science museum on campus, where they looked at plaster casts of dinosaurs, the successive stages of the evolution of man, the growth of a fetus from fertilized egg to full-term infant, Egyptian sarcophagi. The following day it rained, and they spent the afternoon playing gin rummy. In the upstairs hallway rainwater dripped steadily into an enamel basin.

Each night Mike slept with her in Kevin's bed. Since nobody made a secret of the fact that they were sleeping together, Orla wondered why she'd been assigned to Kevin's room in the first place.

Saturday evening before dinner she telephoned her family, using the extension in the den, and her mother said, "I have half a mind to call the police."

"I'm eighteen, Mom. You can't make me go back if I don't want to."

"Have you gone crazy, Orla?"

Orla thought possibly she had. She could not now imagine driving back to Utley, or in September to the small college in Indiana, either. After less than a week she felt completely at home in this rambling, untidy house, which could not have been more different from her own. It was almost as though she'd become quite another person in order to live here.

Later that same evening Mike went somewhere in Meg's Honda, and Meg and Orla sat in the kitchen drinking tea and looking at house magazines. Meg was thinking about redecorating the master bedroom: laying thick wall-to-wall carpeting over the worn floorboards, installing some built-in shelving and storage space, taking down the limp old curtains and hanging draperies with valances, perhaps re-covering a pair of overstuffed chairs that were now in the living room and moving them up in front of the fireplace. She didn't say so, but Orla knew the changes were intended to create a cozy and comfortable place for her husband to die in.

"What do you think, Orla, beige or eggshell for the carpet? Eggshell's more cheery. On the other hand, beige will go longer before showing dirt."

Amazing, Orla thought, that Meg could contemplate these questions without her voice quavering or her eyes filling with tears. Orla was not at all sure that, married to a dying Mike, she'd be so strong.

When he came home that night — twenty past three by the digital clock on Kevin's desk — Orla heard him washing up in the bathroom down the hall. But it was the door to Mike's own room across the way that opened and closed again.

~

In the morning Meg walked into the kitchen wearing a linen dress the color of lemon sherbet. "I'm on my way to church," she said to Orla, who was finishing a bowl of shredded wheat in the breakfast nook. "Why don't you come with me?"

"I'm Catholic."

"Well, I suppose it's the same God. Don't you?"

Orla looked down at the paint-spattered jeans and tee shirt that said, in letters faded from black to gray, WAGASAUKEN WOLVERINES. "I can't go this way."

"Mike must have some decent slacks and a dress shirt you could wear. In our church we aren't very formal, especially in the summer."

Upstairs, Orla knocked gently on Mike's door and then went in. She hadn't been in this room before. Unlike Kevin's, here there was little evidence of eighteen years of growing up: no model airplanes, rock posters, or baseball mitts stiff as carcasses. No record and tape collection. Only a handful of books in the bookcase. Mike slept soundly, his face to the wall.

Orla opened his closet and considered the two or three pairs of pants on wire hangers. One was navy blue — the pair he wore to his high-school graduation, she figured. If they had enough room in the seat they'd be all right. She was pleased to find the striped shirt, now washed and tumble-dried, also hanging there.

For a moment she watched the light summer blanket move gently as he breathed, wishing he'd wake up and see her standing here and lure her into his bed. But he didn't, so she changed her clothes and accompanied Meg to church.

The day was hazy, over eighty degrees at not quite ten in the morning. Meg parked on the street and they walked several blocks to the church, a low brown-shingled structure with spiky iron railings separating the grounds from the sidewalk. The minister, dressed in a long gown, stood in the doorway greeting the arriving parishioners. A spindly man, the minister, with wispy white hair, his palm dry as bread flour. If Orla's attire surprised him, he gave no sign.

Inside, colors were muted and furnishings plain, very different from the church in Utley where Orla had received the rite of baptism and made her first communion, where Christ's body writhed in agony on a wooden cross and painted blood dripped from the wound in his side. No candles flickering in alcoves here, no smell of incense, no confession boxes. Her mother had taught her that worshiping in a Protestant church, even stepping over the threshold, amounted to a mortal sin, and Orla had never done so until now. She half-expected God to smite her right there on the spot. But Meg moved calmly into a pew, and Orla followed.

During the service Orla stood when Meg stood, sat when Meg sat. Mike's slacks felt cool against her legs, the pew cushion sandpapery through the summer-weight material. A parishioner coughed a dry cough. Somewhere a fly buzzed. Orla's mind drifted away from the sermon, to Mike in his strangely empty bedroom. She could not help wondering where he went last night, and why he hadn't slept with her.

At the close of the sermon the congregation murmured the Lord's Prayer, and then brass collection plates were handed around, and they rose for the final hymn. Beautiful words: *Though like the wanderer, the sun gone down, darkness be over me, my rest a stone. Yet in my dreams I'd be nearer, my God, to thee . . .*

"They sang that on the *Titanic*," Meg remarked as they were leaving the church.

That night, after poached salmon and strawberry-rhubarb pie, Mike's favorite dessert, Meg washed the dishes and Orla wielded the towel. With his backpack hitched over one shoulder Mike kissed each of them on the nape of the neck and headed out the screen door. "See you," he said.

They didn't hear the Honda start up. He must have gone on foot. "Tomorrow, or the next day, there'll be a phone call," Meg said, "to let us know he's okay."

Orla kept her cool, though she felt sick to her stomach. She dried a water glass and placed it upside down in the cupboard where it belonged.

"You won't take this personally, will you? Even before he was born Mike was restless, kicking like a little demon, determined to get out."

After a silence Orla said, "Mike can't stand watching his dad stumble."

Meg turned on the tap to rinse a handful of cutlery. "Funny thing about those two. They're so alike, but Jim never could see it."

"How long do you think Mike will be gone?"

Meg shrugged, laid the cutlery in the drainer. "Hard to tell. I hope you'll stay a while, Orla."

"I don't know . . ."

"We kind of rattle around in this big old place, just Jim and I."

Maybe what Meg meant was, she could use a buffer. The next day Orla found a job in town, filing documents in the office of an attorney who practiced personal injury, estate planning, and family law. Brainless though it was, she didn't mind the work. She enjoyed being able to pay for her keep.

To his parents Mike sent postcards from Elkhart, North Platte, Salt Lake City, Seattle. Somebody'd told him there were good summer jobs in Alaska, working on fish-processing boats, and maybe he'd give it a shot. Orla received a postcard, too. "Guess I made that U-turn," it said. "Love . . ." He left it unsigned.

At the end of August Orla moved into a one-room apartment in town and began to take courses at the university, part-time. Every Sunday she came to Hawthorn Street for dinner, except the week Mike was home in between his Alaskan adventure and returning to Ohio for his sophomore year. In October she and Meg turned over the old garden patch, dug a bag of bone meal into the soil, and planted two hundred daffodil bulbs. With any luck they'd bloom before the maple leafed out.

VII

1968–1995

1

WHILE JIM and Peter talked, Meg quartered an apple with a paring knife and laid the sections on her dessert plate. Dreamily she smiled. Perhaps she was listening to them, perhaps thinking her own thoughts, perhaps thinking of nothing. She ate one apple section, then the others, until only a few seeds remained on the plate. No one but Meg could eat an entire apple and leave nothing but the seeds. Her absentminded gluttony made Jim nervous.

She rose, great with child, lumbering in bedroom slippers around the table to clear it. Peter, ever the dutiful guest, stacked plates and carried them to the sink. Jim considered it a plum to have secured Peter Finesilver's friendship; he knew their departure together from the smoky conference room after Thursday afternoon seminars drew the envy of everyone there. Inevitably there'd be a good wine reposing in Peter's briefcase, awaiting Meg's invitation to stay for potluck after a congenial round or two of Dry Sack.

Jim took the wine bottle and his glass into the living room and lit a cigarette. Out in the kitchen their voices were unintelligible under the sound of running water.

He should feel pleased. His seminar paper on the Digby Magdalen had gone over well; the others seemed impressed. On the walk up Broadway to Jim's apartment afterward, Peter had paid a number of generous compliments to the presentation. Jim savored the praise, coming as it did from an Oxford lecturer, already a distinguished medievalist, here on a prestigious one-year fellowship. Persuasive, Peter had said, was Jim's discussion of the problematic second half of the manuscript, in which the Magdalen journeys to the pagan land Marcylle as apostle in atonement for her sins. Jim was not venturing too far out on a limb, in Peter's opinion, to suggest that the work could be termed a miracle play, which would make it perhaps the sole valid miracle play in English to survive the theological carnage of the Reformation. He'd especially enjoyed Jim's identification of Marcylle as Marseilles — dig at the French, fifteenth-century in-joke. Peter's only quibble had been couched in polite British diffidence: *Although it occurs to me to wonder whether you oughtn't to consider . . .*

Trouble was, the quibble was more than a quibble. Sitting here, knocking back what was left of Peter's Bordeaux, Jim suspected that the query went right to the core of his argument, exposing its essential squishiness. Peter was absolutely right, damn it. Miracle play or not, nowhere in the paper did Jim address the real problem posed by the manuscript: the frequent apparent confounding of the Magdalen with the Virgin Mary in that half of the play. Sure, the Magdalen had plenty to atone for. But the Virgin? How could you take the play seriously as a coherent whole when such confusions existed, unaccounted for? Where was the dramatic unity? The play, at least the second half, might be the botched result of later emendation, or even a mistaken conjoining of two separate manuscripts.

Good of Peter not to have raised the issue during the seminar, but to save it for the private, chilly walk. He could really have nailed Jim if he'd chosen to.

Low laughter in the kitchen. Fleetingly Jim wondered what the two of them found to talk about out there. He upended the wine bottle and emptied it into his glass. Shit. The paper might be publishable, somewhere, somehow, but not until he'd solved the conundrum of the strangely interwoven Magdalen/Virgin identities was it going to come remotely close to establishing his reputation. He'd been counting on it to propel him out in front of that crew of mud sharks and cave dwellers, his fellow graduate students. Little hope of that now unless Peter should take an interest, come up with an idea or two. He certainly had the time on his fancy endowed vacation; it wasn't as though he had two sections of clueless undergraduates to teach each semester.

Absently Jim listened to silverware clinking, the tap being turned on and off, Meg's and Peter's murmuring voices like distantly cooing doves. The Bordeaux was sour after fruit and cake, and the cigarette didn't taste so great, either. He knew his hair and clothes reeked of other people's smoke after the seminar. What he really needed was a shower and a good night's sleep, but both would be hard to come by: the dishwashing having consumed most of the hot water in the tank, Meg's clumsy body so huge in the bed, hogging the blanket, the Digby Magdalen swirling around in his brain. All at once he decided to take a walk.

Without letting them know, he grabbed his duffel coat from the hook in the hall and left by the front door. He pictured them coming into the living room, Meg's face still flushed with steam from the dishpan, and finding his chair empty. Let them wonder, he thought, flinging his lit cigarette end into a bush.

◆

She'd been a student in the Chaucer survey last spring, Jim's fourth semester of T.A.-ing that course. A senior with honey-colored hair curling down her back, a little overweight, velvety dark eyes, an enticingly innocent smile. One April afternoon she came to see him in his office hours, and he took her out for coffee afterward, not on campus, but to a place in town where they served bitter black coffee in acorn-sized cups, and paperback copies of Sartre or Camus, their front covers missing and spines broken, got left behind on the tables. Sure, there was the unspoken law against dating students who depended on you for their grades. But for some reason Jim had an almost insatiable bed lust that spring, and she was so goddamn willing, and before he knew it, fucking her dominated his thoughts to a degree that was almost scary.

He knew he should be sublimating, directing his energies toward doing significant original scholarship that would catch Professor Bulloch's eye. Instead he'd invite her to his room and give her a glass of the cheap sherry he kept in a bookcase and then take her clothes off and spread her luxurious honey curls out on the pillow before delving into her. In June, just before he was about to take off for a summer in Avignon and Bruges, Meg tearfully confessed that she was pregnant. Never mind that she was on the Pill and swore she'd never missed taking a single one. After anguishing over the situation for a couple of weeks, his suitcases half packed, he cashed in his airplane ticket and they found this hot, crummy apartment, and he taught a summer course and slaved in the library, and she worked in a shop that sold hash pipes and incense, and they fought and she cried and he shouted and stormed out and came back and at the end of the summer they married in the county courthouse, both of them too exhausted to think what else to do.

During her pregnancy Meg gained weight, not only in her belly but in her breasts and thighs and upper arms. In September he brought his new wife with him to Bulloch's little party for his advisees, during which she sat on a spindly-legged chair, the teacup jiggling on its saucer in her hand, and seemed to fall into a doze or coma in the overheated room. He'd been terrified she was going to break the chair with her weight or drop the cup and saucer, shattering both into a thousand pieces, her milky tea spreading into a large, indelible stain on Old Bullshit's Oriental carpet. Nothing happened, but after that he went to such parties alone.

⟋

After half an hour of aimless walking in the cold night air, which was windy enough that he'd pulled up the hood of his duffel coat, Jim found himself on Ellingham, a street name he recognized from the mimeographed list of department faculty. The alliteration of the address had struck him: 11½ Ellingham, like something out of the sort of English novel you find in a serious used-book store. It belonged, he knew, to an angular assistant professor who wore silver earrings in her pierced ears and whose dark hair was clipped short in a fashion that seemed European or from some other era. In the faculty mail room she made acerbic remarks, quickly riffling through the messages in her box and throwing most of them in the trash. Assistant Professor Christine Hartshorn, Ph.D., from Princeton. There were lights on at 11½, a narrow town house sort of deal with a little front garden, now nothing but frozen stalks behind an iron fence. Jim stood in the street smoking, picturing her up late grading papers, or working on an article. He thought he might run Peter's query by her. Anyway, couldn't hurt to establish a contact among the faculty who were actively publishing, unlike Old Bullshit. He dropped his cigarette and squashed it under his shoe.

The gate squeaked as he opened it, whined shut, and clanged as he closed the latch. A cat from somewhere flew by, startling him, and scrambled under a bush. He mounted the three steps and pressed his finger on the buzzer.

"Who is it?" she said from inside. He faced the peephole and yelled his name, wondered whether she'd recognize it — whether she'd open the door, even if she did. He imagined his face blown up and distorted, all forehead or bulging cheeks, by the peephole glass. Then he heard the bolt slide and the lock turn.

Stumbling over his words he explained that he'd been passing by, noticed her lights on, thought she might be able to help him with a problem. A dark brow arched quizzically. A problem? The cat took this opportunity to leap out of the bush and streak into the open doorway. Behind her he could hear classical music of some sort — Stravinsky, he guessed.

"I was about to quit for the night," she said. "I guess you could come in for a minute."

She took the record off the turntable, blew dust from it, and slipped it into its jacket. Meanwhile he eyed various possible surfaces on which to sit. A leather couch was heaped with books and manuscripts; a butterfly chair looked too awkward to climb out of once you were in it. "Nightcap?" she said. Without waiting for a reply she padded away on bare feet into some distant part of the house.

He stood before the fireplace, contemplating the postcards propped against an old gilt-framed mirror. Museum cards: a Brancusi marble, a Seurat, a Hiroshige composition of birds in flight with eddying calligraphy. Enamel vases on either end of the mantel contained wheatlike sheaves of grass and dry stems supporting small purplish lanternlike pods. He could not imagine Meg finding such arrangements attractive. In the flecked, hazy mirror, he looked disconcertingly boyish: mussed straight hair on his forehead, eyes watery from windburn.

She returned with a bottle and a couple of tumblers, shoved

some papers to one side of her desk with her elbow, and poured a small amount of whiskey into each glass. The drink smelled like paint thinner and felt worse in this throat; by dint of will he kept himself from choking.

"What's the problem you wanted to talk about?" she asked. She lifted her glass to take a sip, and the loose black jersey she was wearing fell away from her neck so that he could see the sharp definition of her collarbone. A single silver bracelet circled her wrist. "A fight with your wife?"

Wife? What made her assume he had a wife? He explained that it was a literary problem, a seminar paper he'd been working on, a discussion of the Digby Magdalen. He'd been assured that the paper was publishable, but he had a nagging suspicion that there were issues he hadn't dealt with sufficiently to get it past the reviewers. Not that he wished to impinge upon her time, but . . .

"I can't say I've given the Digby Magdalen much thought," she said. "If any."

He wondered what her breasts would be like under the jersey. Small, firm as figs. Dark nipples. Maybe a mole centered on the bone between them. The drink was going to his head, and he needed to sit down. Where, though? She didn't seem uncomfortable leaning against the desk, her bare heels lifted from the floor just enough to let her rest her butt on the edge, her legs in smooth tight pants making a v-shaped prop for her body. A paper slid off the desk, caught an air current, and landed under a chair.

"However," she went on, "I guess I could take a look at it sometime."

He muttered inarticulate thanks. She looked at him over the rim of her glass, as if expecting him to say something else, but the way to proceed eluded him. His head felt muddled. He must have been more down than he'd realized by the stress of the seminar paper, and other pressures in his life.

Finally she said, "When you get a chance, leave it in my box in the department."

The cat came in from the shadowy hallway and mewed. Both ears had been chewed off in fights, and one eye was sewn shut.

"Well," she said. "I have a nine o'clock class tomorrow morning." She screwed the cap on the whiskey bottle.

Before he knew it he was out the door, dazedly stepping on a paved walk slippery with frost, tussling with the gate latch, sorting out which direction he'd come from and what would be the best way back to Farnum Street.

～

The apartment was dark when Jim entered it, dark but unbearably hot; Meg must have neglected to turn down the thermostat again. He groped for the tinny box on the wall and with his thumb pushed the dial all the way to the left. In response the churning furnace died. By now the whiskey had mostly worn off, but not his edgy excitement. Why in the name of God hadn't he handled Christine Hartshorn more deftly? She'd been waiting for him to make a move, he felt sure of it now, and he'd just stood there like a jerk.

He found the glass half full of the dregs of Peter's wine, which remained on the coffee table where Jim had left it. He finished it off in a couple of swallows. Stuff tasted terrible, and not enough alcohol content to do anything for the jumpiness, anyhow. He remembered that Meg had some el cheapo brandy she had used to douse her Christmas fruitcakes with — as if any of the lucky recipients would ever eat the wretched things. He went down the hall into the kitchen and turned on the light. After rooting around for a while in a cupboard jammed with dented cans of pineapple slices and half-empty jelly jars, the contents of which had crystallized, he finally found the brandy bottle. Meg was not the best housekeeper in the world, or the best cook, either. He filled the wineglass with brandy, turned off the light, and stood at the kitchen window to drink it.

A fuzzy moon had risen beyond the back porch. Jim could see shadowy forms: last summer's geraniums dead in their pots; folded metal lawn chairs — already, he knew, speckled with rust; a hibachi he'd bought in a drugstore for a Fourth of July barbecue, also rusting. Still pinned to the line that she'd strung across the porch hung a dishrag or some article of clothing, stiff with frost. He knew he'd be in bad shape for the Brit Lit survey section he had to teach in the morning. Right now he didn't care. He drank all the brandy in the glass and stumbled into the bedroom and shucked his clothes. Under the covers he pressed his cheek to Meg's back, tangled himself in her silky web of hair. She sighed, but didn't awaken.

∽

Not the next day — that would seem overeager — but Monday of the following week, Jim left his seminar paper in Christine Hartshorn's box. To his annoyance he noted that his hand shook a little as he poked it in among her mail and notices. She was, after all, only an untenured assistant professor, even if she did have a Princeton Ph.D., and held no direct control over his fate as a graduate student. Moreover, he wasn't so sure whether he wanted to start something with her, now that he considered the matter in the cold light of day. Christine was no gawky, cow-eyed undergraduate. She might add more complexity to his life than he really wished to deal with at the moment.

Still, he hadn't expected a three-week wait for the paper to return to his box. When he happened to see her in the hall, or striding briskly across campus, or eating lunch with another faculty member, she seemed distracted. Her eyes did not meet his. Jim found himself checking his box after class, whenever he went to the communal coffee maker in the department kitchen, first thing in the morning and last thing before leaving the building late in the afternoon. Finally he found the paper amid some overdue student essays on "The Wife of Bath's Tale," looking somewhat rumpled, as though she'd carried it around in her briefcase most of the time since he'd given it to her. He thought it had a faint smell of leather about it, or some other dry, astringent scent he couldn't identify.

She'd penciled a few comments in the margins: *sentence slightly garbled; point could use some development; significance??* To his shame, she'd even corrected the spelling of a couple of words and circled a typo. But as to the issue that Peter suggested might be a potential death trap, nothing.

Jim thought of taking the paper to her office and raising it with her. He pictured himself sitting in a straight-backed, armless chair next to Christine's desk, in the same situation as the undergraduate supplicants in his own office, and couldn't bring himself to do it.

～

Meg gave birth in January, during the thaw, icicles dripping from the eaves of the apartment house. In the delivery room at four in the morning he held his child, a boy, in his arms, and felt . . . not joy, exactly, but pumped up with adrenaline and racked with fatigue after the interminable labor. His eyes filled with tears. Yet he was aware that some part of him was standing in a far corner of the chaotic, blood-soaked hospital room, coolly watching himself nestle this unlooked- and unasked-for being in the crook of his arm.

They named the baby Kevin, although Jim would have preferred something more unusual, with a ring to it. However, Kevin had been Meg's brother's name. The year before the young medic had walked into a land mine somewhere in the Mekong delta. Jim could summon no argument that outweighed that fact. Anyway, he had more immediately compelling problems to worry about: his comprehensives coming up in April; whether his assistantship would be renewed and if not how the hell he was going to earn a living for the three of them; how to get enough sleep with the baby squalling all the time. Out of desperation he bought an old down mummy bag in an army surplus store and slept in it most nights on his office floor. He had to pick the shed feathers out of the carpeting and secrete the bedroll before seven in the morning, when the first of the three T.A.'s he shared his office with arrived. And all day he'd be sore in every muscle and joint, so it hardly paid.

Several times that spring, strolling up Broadway or over Dry Sack, he mentioned to Peter that soon he'd have to hammer out the prospectus for his dissertation. He was considering expanding the Digby Magdalen seminar paper, but as Peter well knew, there was the problem of the Magdalen/Virgin confusion . . . Peter never took the hint, simply went merrily on scribbling about the Wakefield Corpus Christi cycle. Goddammit, Old Bullshit was probably going to kick the bucket before Jim got the dissertation halfway done, let alone completed.

Kevin was fussiest, always, at the precise moment they sat down to supper. Meg began the habit of bringing the baby to the table to nurse while she ate with fork and fingers. Jim didn't care, since the shrill wailing ceased, at least temporarily, although his mother would have been horrified if she were on the scene: Meg's naked breast overflowing with milk, the grease on her chin shining in the light of the ceiling fixture, the greedily suckling infant, the noisy rooting-piglet sounds.

Something made Jim recall the Bible story of Moses, escaped from Egypt, gazing on his firstborn son and saying to his wife, "I have been a stranger in a strange land." Everywhere is a strange land, Jim thought. Where can you escape to?

2

Jim had chosen the restaurant because it looked pleasant, not too expensive, and right across the street from the small hotel near Russell Square where he was staying. He wasn't sure why he'd called Peter, almost hadn't. Nearly six years since he'd seen Peter Finesilver, Oxford don, though once in a while Jim glanced through the self-consciously witty little air letters his old friend sent. God knew why they were still in touch. Meg's doing. She didn't grasp that he and Peter had for some time been on different scholarly tracks, parallel lines that would never again converge. Still, he'd found the prospect of spending his last evening in London in his cramped, stingily heated, and dimly lit hotel room less than inviting, and at the last minute asked the desk clerk to put the call through to the six-digit Oxford number Meg had written in his date book before he left for England.

Jim picked up the menu — Greek specialties, though tamed by British taste and sensibilities, and the difficulties of acquiring fresh provisions, especially now, when the sun scarcely struggled above the horizon in this northern clime — and thought he'd probably have the taramasalata, followed by . . . and then Peter materialized, apologizing for being late, bomb scare in the tube, the IRA most likely . . .

"Good of you to come all this way," Jim said.

"Not at all," Peter replied. "My pleasure." He left again to stow his wet umbrella and raincoat on the rack near the door, returned to the table, and shook Jim's hand. "You've become a father again since I've seen you," he said. "Congratulations."

Was this a put-down? Jim wondered. The sum of his accomplishment in Peter's eyes. He said, "Well, those things happen," and Peter smiled and accepted a menu from the waiter.

"I ordered a carafe of the house red," Jim said. "Not retsina, hope you don't mind. Can't stand the stuff."

"The house red will do very well," Peter said, lowering his eyes to examine the menu.

He looked the same, yet not the exactly the same. Eyebrows bushier, nose assuming a larger importance or mission. A fleshy bump beside one nostril that Jim didn't recall. The usual British failure with teeth: slightly yellow, crowded, signaling future quiet crises in the nether regions. They loved their sweets, the Brits, and the National Health Service didn't, apparently, believe in preventive dentistry. Pluck 'em all out, issue a standard set of store teeth, save everybody a lot of trouble. "Yes, two sons now," Jim said. "Kevin and Michael. Mike cut his first tooth last week. A trial for us all, believe me."

Peter unfolded his napkin, placed it in his lap. "And how is Meg?" he asked.

"She's . . . oh, you know, busy with the kids . . ." The waiter brought the wine, and poured it from the carafe into their glasses. Murky, tarry-looking stuff. After Peter's tediously close questioning of the waiter as to ingredients, they gave their orders: taramasalata and lamb kabobs for Jim, vegetable soup and some sort of casserole for Peter.

"I suppose you heard about Bulloch," Jim said when the waiter departed.

"Yes. Someone sent me the obituary from the *Times*."

"I thought sure he'd keel over in the middle of my dissertation. That's one reason I decided to move out of the medieval stuff."

"You never did anything more with the Digby Magdalen?" Bland expression behind the wire-frame lenses.

"Shelved it," Jim said. "I began to suspect that insofar as there were going to be jobs at all, Renaissance drama was where they would be. Chaucer might get pitched out of the curriculum, but it'd be a while before they'd find the courage to dispense with the Old Bard. I ended up writing on Fletcher."

"Which play?" Peter asked.

"*The Wilde Goose Chase,* aptly enough."

While they were waiting for the starters, as Peter called them, to arrive, Jim told him about the school in northcentral New Jersey where he was assistant professor: formerly Wagasauken Junior College, now Wagasauken University, referred to by students and faculty alike as Godforsaken U. Might as well make a comedy out of it, defuse Peter's scorn. Big sprawling department, chronically underfunded and short-staffed, the literature people squeezed by the tech writing people, hordes of part-time lecturers straggling in and out, the students mostly commuters. Only two guys doing Tudor drama, himself and a half-senile old coot who ought to have retired aeons ago. Last spring he'd been landed with teaching Chaucer while the Chaucer man was on sabbatical, and Jim had found his Middle English uncomfortably rusty, he didn't mind saying. Up for tenure next year. Of course he had applications in other places — couldn't imagine spending the rest of his life in exile in Jersey — but the shitty job market . . . Sometimes he wished he'd acceded to his father's plea and gone into engineering.

The Oxford don nodded sympathetically, helped himself to a flabby English roll from the bread basket, and tugged it open over his plate. "Have you given up cigarettes?" Peter asked.

Observant of him. "Result of a bargain."

"With Meg?"

"With God."

"God?" Peter asked, his prickle-bush brows aloft. First time the subject of God had ever risen between them, though of course there'd been plenty of conversations touching on the knottier vexations of medieval doctrine as it influenced the literature of the period.

"If He'd get me through my comps I'd quit smoking. A joke, but I thought I'd better stick to my side of the contract. Just in case." Jim tried the wine, on which floated bits of cork and other debris. Had presence, you could say that for it. "Anyway, I've taken up running." He went on to talk about the five miles around the cindery track on campus every morning before breakfast, the problems with his knee. Forced to wear an Ace bandage most of the time, was wearing one now, as a matter of fact. Still, what was a little pain compared with the high? Peter should try it, Jim advised, though he didn't imagine for a second that he would. Too much the sedentary scholar, wedded to his dusty carrel.

The first course came, along with salads composed of limp lettuce topped by pallid wedges of tomato, and for the moment they devoted themselves to the food. When he'd finished his taramasalata Jim pushed the plate aside and said, "Tell me, Peter. What's your news?" expecting he'd be treated to the latest philological enthusiasm, perhaps even an announcement of a forthcoming monograph publication.

Peter hesitated long enough for Jim to wonder whether there'd been some recent glitch in the Oxford don's brilliant career and then said, "I'm to be married. In April."

"Well," Jim said. He'd always thought of Peter as being avuncularly asexual, or perhaps even a closet queer — although he'd learned by now that Englishmen could fool you. "This calls for a toast," he said, picking up his glass. "To the happy couple." He raised the glass to Peter and drank. "Who is she?"

"Enid's an attorney. Here in the City."

"Well," Jim said again, even more surprised. He'd envisioned another scholar. Dowdy clothes, wire-framed glasses like Peter's, a female version of him complete with hairy eyebrows. "How'd you meet her?"

Peter sipped the strong, gritty wine. "Through a mutual friend, about a year ago. We became engaged in the fall."

How measured, Jim thought. Civilized. Rather different from his own engagement, if you could call it that, the horrible summer of Meg's tears and his sweat, culminating in the trip to the courthouse when she still had one dress left she could get buttoned and the celebration afterward in the backyard, a bunch of grad students pouring beer on one another and grinding potato chips into the crabgrass, "Lucy in the Sky with Diamonds" blasting out of the stereo on the porch, both he and Meg ending up skunk-drunk, screwing on the dirty kitchen floor while the remnants of the party carried on in the waning light.

"I haven't written to Meg about it yet," Peter went on. He submitted to the removal of his soup bowl, in spite of its being still half full of canned string beans and corn kernels, and wiped his mouth with his napkin. He seemed embarrassed or nervous, picking up his dessert spoon and absently polishing the bowl with his thumb.

"She'll be pleased," Jim said. "She's fond of you."

And then he saw it in Peter's face, as clearly as if the man had shouted it across the table: there'd been something more than *fond*ness between him and Meg — on his side, at least. Well, goddamn. Jim finished his wine and splashed some more into the glass. Magnanimity would be the way to go: Quite all right, old boy, don't let it trouble you, we're all adults here. But he remembered Peter's blithe disinclination to help him with the Digby Magdalen, a failure of friendship that now seemed a form of treachery. So Jim said, "Just as you've been fond of her. Quite a few letters postmarked Oxford, over the years."

"They were addressed to you, as well. I could not help noticing that Meg was the only one who answered them."

"That's what wives are for. You'll find out."

"I expect," Peter said, as though looking thoughtfully into his future and weighing his own nature and habits against those of other men, "I'll continue to manage my own correspondence, even after my marriage." Nevertheless, there was an edge to the remark.

"Including to Meg?"

"Including to you both."

"I'd be honored," Jim said, not bothering to hide his sarcasm.

Peter laid down the dessert spoon. "Very well," he said. "The truth is that if for some reason you and Meg had chosen to part, I would not have been sorry."

"I get the picture. Over here biding your time. Sticking pins in a Jim doll."

"But then," Peter continued, ignoring his crack, "Meg wrote that she was expecting another child."

Jim stared at him. What if he were to tell him that Mike had been a mistake, as Kevin had been, not a forgotten pill this time but a pinprick hole in a diaphragm? Hell, no. Let the Oxford don think he'd been chasing a chimera, that the Mowbry marriage was one made in heaven. "Hence," Jim said, "the engagement to Miss What's-Her-Name."

"Not at all."

"No? Timing's suspiciously coincidental." He could hear himself slurring his words. Better take it easy on the wine. Peter opened his mouth to say something, but the waiter arrived with Jim's kabobs and Peter's mucky grayish casserole. "What the hell *is* that?" Jim asked.

"Moussaka. Aubergines. What you Americans call eggplant."

Rapidly Jim consumed the meat from one whole skewer. Then he said, "Maybe I don't fully grasp how things are done over here, but this engagement doesn't seem like a very square deal — from the lady's point of view."

"How so?"

"If you don't love her . . ."

"I didn't say I don't love her," Peter said stiffly.

"But not the way you love my wife. Life is tough, hey, Peter?"

They ate in silence now. The restaurant had nearly filled during their meal, the noise level grown too high to talk over with any ease, given the direction the conversation had taken. Smoke from the table next to theirs silted over them, and Jim realized he was hot, stifling, when generally in this miserable country he froze to death.

The waiter appeared at Peter's elbow. "Coffee for you, sirs? Dessert?"

"Yes, I'll have coffee," Jim said. "Black."

"I think I won't," Peter said. He looked at his watch and extracted a ten-pound note from his billfold, which he placed on the table along with his napkin.

"No, dinner's on me. My invitation."

Peter smiled faintly. "I nearly didn't come." Leaving the banknote where it was, he rose and said, "Please give my best to Meg."

"I will," Jim replied, but he did no such thing. In fact, he never mentioned to Meg that he'd seen Peter in London, and apparently Peter didn't write to her about the meeting, either. In April came the announcement of his marriage to Enid Elspeth Strudwick — a name to send a shiver down your spine. Meg ran out and bought an expensive something-or-other and insisted that Jim sign his name next to hers on the card.

3

Jim did his stretches against the side of the house, focusing, as he did every morning, on the paint that was coming off the boards in bubbled scrofulous sheddings, in spite of his having paid a fortune last summer — or was it the summer before? — to have the whole house scraped and painted by an army of oafs hired out of the student employment office at an exorbitant sum per hour, the subsidizing of the hapless underskilled by the exploited underpaid. Today he was going to contact the siding company that had been bugging him by telephone and have the problem taken care of once and for all, never mind if it cost the better part of a month's salary.

He untied and removed his running shoes in the back entryway. Foul smell coming from the half-bath that one of the house's former owners had jerry-built into the rear entrance. Toilet breakdown, again, or cat box badly needed changing. He slung his jacket on top of one of the other coats hanging on the overloaded hooks, stepped into his moccasins, and opened the kitchen door.

"Running late," Meg said from the sink. Mike was still in his high chair, bib and curling fair hair stuccoed with oatmeal. "Before you go in the shower, maybe you could help Kevin find his homework paper?"

Jim didn't know why this household needed to be so chaotic all the time. The homes of his colleagues seemed to run with calm efficiency, even though some of the wives had outside jobs. Plants watered, children fed, toys picked up and put away, drinks served at civilized hours in unspotted glasses with Scarlatti playing in the background and the brats stashed somewhere out of sight. Not here. Meg couldn't seem to get it together, and you couldn't blame her job, only part-time, filing records down in the bowels of Alumni Hall, work she didn't need to take home with her, work a cretin would not have to devote full attention to. Yet in this house the kitchen floor hadn't been mopped in six months, parts of busted toys were everywhere, the cats had free rein of the countertops until he tossed them off. The table in the breakfast nook was loaded with cereal boxes, old copies of *Family Circle*, crayons, dirty dishes. Find a homework paper in this mess? Forget it. Jim thought about the Augean Stables and wondered whether his own sin could possibly have been egregious enough to deserve this fate.

Mike had begun to whimper and pull at the harness that fastened him into the high chair. Jim wiped his son's face and hair with the washcloth, unbuckled him, and lifted him out. Sturdy little bottom, a solid heft to it. The boy clung to Jim's sweatshirt, his plump fingers gripping the material. "Poppy," he said, and thumped his stockinged feet against Jim's midsection. One sock was striped, the other polka-dotted. "Dansu," Mike said.

"Dansu? What is that, Japanese?"

"Dansu," Mike repeated, insistently bobbing his head as if to make a pony giddyap.

"Oh, *dan*su. Well, let's see." Jim began a waltz, like he'd been taught in Miss Wright's Wednesday afternoon dance classes back in Dayton a million years ago. Holding Mike close to his chest, the kid drooling on his sweatshirt, Jim waltzed around the kitchen table, past tricycles and other clutter in the hallway, into the living room. Dim in there, lacy curtains against shades drawn all the way down, the one calm spot in the house. For once the kid didn't wriggle to be set free. Gracefully they glided to the Viennese waltz Jim hummed, and Mike nestled his head into Jim's neck.

"Jim?" came Meg's voice from one of the close-smelling, untidy bedrooms upstairs. "What time is it? Where's Kevin? Have you found his homework paper yet?"

~

He'd never paid much attention to her except to notice that she carried a big black artist's portfolio around with her as well as the usual satchel full of textbooks and papers. Also, she seemed less scattered than most of the rest of the part-time faculty, who were always tearing from class to class like the frazzled White Rabbit on his way down the hole. Her short auburn hair was inevitably combed smoothly close to her face, her clothes stylishly neat, her expression serene. But he didn't know her name or even what she lectured in. One afternoon in March he was on his way back to the department from the library, where he'd been working on a conference paper, and he saw her sitting on a bench. Too chilly to be sitting there, he thought, and then he realized she was noiselessly weeping into a tissue. If there was one thing that drove him nuts it was a woman in tears, and he fully intended to hurry on past as though he hadn't seen her. Nevertheless, he found himself leaving the path and taking a seat on the bench.

For quite a while neither of them said anything. Jim watched a squirrel run halfway down the trunk of an oak, stare at them beadily, leap from the tree, and skitter away through last fall's leaves. Several students came down the path, including a kid who'd cut Jim's nine o'clock Shakespeare class. Spotting Jim, he shrugged his neck guiltily inside his Wagasauken sweatshirt and hurried on by. A sudden gust buffeted the black portfolio that leaned against the bench, and Jim grabbed it to keep it from falling over.

The lecturer snuffled. "I didn't mean to make a public spectacle of myself," she said. He muttered something about doubting that anyone — aside from himself — had noticed that she was making a public spectacle of herself and asked if there was something he could do. She refolded the tissue to find a dry spot. "I suppose you could kill the rat for me."

Which rat? Jim wondered. Was this common knowledge around the department that he'd somehow missed hearing about? The chair, perhaps, taking advantage of a lowly part-timer? Jim wouldn't put it past the arrogant sonofabitch. Through leafless branches he looked up into a gruel-colored sky, felt the wind scouring him through his topcoat. What she needed, he told her, was a drink.

"I can't let people see me looking like this."

Jim racked his brain. Ridiculous to take her out to Hawthorn Street, drag her into the grubby kitchen and pop a can of Bud for her while Meg stirred pots, Mike hurled bits of hot dog onto the floor, and *Sesame Street* blared in the background.

"You could come to my place," she said. "I think I have some gin."

~

She lived in a remote area of the campus near the steam plant, in high-rise junior faculty housing hastily thrown together out of concrete and glass during the sixties, when Wagasauken was transmogrifying itself into a so-called university. On the ride she'd revealed that her name was Sarah Radetzky, an ABD from NYU who was teaching two sections of intermediate composition while working on her dissertation. What's with the portfolio? Jim wanted to know. Oh, as an employee of the university she got a free course, so she was taking one in drawing. No, she didn't consider herself an artist. She liked to draw, that was all. Jim had found her modesty charming, been pleased she seemed to be cheering up.

He heard water running in the bathroom, looked around her living room while he waited for her to return with the gin, a shot of which he could use himself, right about now. Tasteful Scandinavian walnut furniture; a few framed prints on the walls; one of those six-foot-high indoor trees with shiny leaves growing near the sliding glass door that led to a balcony. Jim noticed a museum postcard tucked into one of the picture frames: Etruscan sarcophagus from the Louvre. Suddenly he remembered the collection of museum cards on Christine Hartshorn's mantel. At the end of the year she'd left for an associate professorship at Smith.

Sarah carried a tray into the room and set it on the coffee table. Bottle of Beefeater, Schweppes tonic, a wedge of ripe Brie, flaky little white crackers on a china plate. The girl may have been sexually exploited, but at least she wasn't hurting for money. "I'll let you fix the drinks," she said.

They sat on the sofa and talked about the new academic vice president and his half-assed task force on which Jim was forced to serve and other aimless chitchat; he noted no tensing of neck or facial muscles when the name of any department member was mentioned. A few cracker crumbs landed on the front of her nubbly chocolate brown sweater, and, like an affectionately heedful parent, he flicked them off for her.

"I feel so much better," she said.

He mentioned that he'd been aware of her around the department, how she never looked as if she'd just locked her keys in her office or left some crucial possession on the bus, like all the other part-timers. She smiled, arranging Brie on a cracker and handing it to him. He ate the cheese slowly enough to savor the creamy, slightly rotten aftertaste. He'd waited years for a situation like this to come along, and he was going to enjoy every goddamn minute, if it killed him.

That night Jim made love to Meg more attentively than he had in many a moon. At eight the next morning a crew piled out of a van and began to install vinyl siding over flaking paint on the leeward side of the house.

4

Arriving home from a stint at the library, around half-past one on an October Saturday afternoon, Jim rounded the corner onto Hawthorn and saw that their garbage cans had been dragged out to the grass strip by the side of the road. Sharp objects like coat hangers and curtain rods poked out of them. Next to the cans were several supermarket boxes, also apparently stuffed with junk. A floor lamp that had graced his boyhood home in Dayton, and been cast in their direction when they married, leaned tipsily against the pile of trash, its frayed cord trailing into the gutter.

Clearly Meg had been seized with a passion to do some heavy cleaning while, all oblivious, Jim gazed into the computer screen in his carrel. Of course. He should have been priming himself for some upheaval right about now, since her second bird had recently left the nest. They'd joked about how Meg's metamorphoses inevitably coincided with the kids' milestones. When Mike started kindergarten she went on an implacable diet and lost thirty pounds. The summer after Kevin graduated from eighth grade she dug up the backyard and turned a scraggly touch-football field into a vegetable garden. The year Kevin went off to Antioch she quit working on campus and took a full-time job downtown. But clean the house? Surely that was going too far.

He left the Honda in the driveway and went into the house the back way. Meg sat in the breakfast nook, eating a sandwich. The kitchen radio was tuned to the Saturday afternoon opera, Puccini by the sound of it, and she'd poured herself a glass of ale. Most unusual for her to drink at midday, especially in the middle of a major project. "What's going on?" he said.

And then he saw it, next to the napkin holder on the table: a ragged pile of letters, some in hotel envelopes, intermingled with folded notes that had been written on department memo stationery. Before this morning they'd been held together with a rubber band and secreted in the hall closet behind a humidifier that hadn't been used since the time Mike had the croup. A convenient hiding place. He could easily add to the stack, or take them into the john with him for purposes of rereading and savoring some of the more agitated passages, written when he and Annie were still tottering deliciously on the brink of their affair.

"Rule number one," Meg said. "Never save things like this."

God, she was cool. Her hair was tucked under the kerchief she'd used to keep dust out of it while cleaning; her eyes were dry.

Well, maybe it's going to be okay, he thought. Maybe she'll laugh it off. The last thing he needed was some big emotional deal right now. Already he felt tired, as though it were the end of term, and they were only five weeks into the semester.

"Meg —"

"This *Annie,* is she your first? Or the most recent in a long line of —"

"Meg, don't —"

"No. I really am curious."

He switched off the opera, shoved aside some magazines on the bench, and sat across from her. How quiet the house was suddenly. For once no pipes banged, or shower ran, or hard rock pounded through the ceiling. No dryer thumped in the basement or underfoot cat whined to be fed. The silence was like the times he'd left the carrel and driven home and walked about the house for a while before realizing he'd forgotten to remove his earplugs.

Meg looked at him across the worn oilcloth, with its sticky rings. "Well?"

"She's not the first," he said.

Meg nodded. Her partly eaten sandwich lay on the plate. Tuna fish. Smelly. He was starving — had eaten nothing since a 6:00 A.M. breakfast. But he could see it wouldn't do to start slicing the loaf of bread that sat going stale on the counter, poking around in the fridge for deli meat. She might jump up from the table and seize the bread knife and carve out his heart.

"How many?"

He shrugged. "The occasional graduate student, nothing serious. Two or three that have been more . . ."

She pulled at her wedding ring in the absentminded way that had long been her habit, as far as the knuckle and back, as far as the knuckle and back. Maybe she'd been doing it since the day they were married. ". . . Serious?"

"Not really. It's not as though I ever thought of breaking up the family, or anything."

"Uh-huh." She turned this over in her mind. "What did *they* think, these women?"

Again he shrugged. "I never told them anything different."

"But what did they *think* was going to happen?"

"I'm not a mind reader, Meg."

"Obviously neither of us is."

"Meg, I want you to know that I always was very careful to protect you."

"Protect me?"

"From" — he found himself almost gagging over the word — "disease."

"And yourself, too, incidentally."

He kept waiting for her to cry, or scream. Now he almost wished she *would* leap up to the counter and grab the bread knife so he could wrest it away from her, maybe getting himself cut, a superficial wound, and she'd weep over his blood dripping onto the linoleum, and bandage the injury for him, and they'd end up making love, right here amid his blood, and it would all blow over. Her calm was making him nervous. He noticed that his hand felt numb, as though he'd been using it to make some repetitive motion that called for the use of unaccustomed muscles, and on his lap he flexed and unflexed his fingers. From outside came a slow mesmerizing scratching, their neighbor on the north side raking leaves.

"Well, I've reached a decision, sitting here" — she glanced at the expensive gold watch he gave her several Christmases ago — "in the hour or so since I stumbled on your little cache."

He thought she was about to tell him she'd be on the phone to their lawyer first thing Monday morning, and he'd better hire his own, because this wasn't going to be friendly. But she didn't say

anything, and it occurred to him that the reason for her unchar-
acteristic composure might be that she didn't give a shit. That she
was actually glad to have an excuse to shed him, take the money
and run. He remembered Peter Finesilver, the Oxford don, now
Professor Peter Finesilver, sitting across from him in the smoky
restaurant, that chilly, rainy evening, in chilly, rainy, godforsaken
England, and confessing that he was in love with Jim's wife.

"I'm going to have my tubes tied," Meg said.

Tubes? Jim thought of the London tube, tube worms that live
on the ocean floor, the tubes inside the Motorola TV in the house
in Dayton when he was growing up.

"I don't," Meg said deliberately, "want to take even the tiniest
risk of starting another life. With you."

Well, this was absurd. Their kids grown, or nearly so, and she
on the verge of menopause, probably, which was what this crazed
housecleaning was all about, as a matter of fact . . . What was the
point? And yet he had to admit that the impact of her words was
worse than if she'd threatened to set a pack of lawyers on him. A
dull, heavy pain had begun somewhere in his chest. He felt his
eyes sting and thought, oh, Jesus, he was going to be the one to
cry. As though she were contemplating a fascinatingly repulsive
bug on a bean plant, she watched tears run down his cheeks.

Then she said, "I think it's too late to be sorry now, if that's
what you are," and took the remains of her lunch to the sink.
With two fingers she pushed the sandwich down the drain and
ran the disposal till it stopped laboring, then went upstairs.

～

He turned the map this way and that, struggling to match it up
with the twists and bends the back road was taking and with the
instructions in the *Guide to the Best Country Inns* that lay open in
his lap. November, dusk approaching, the drizzle that had fallen

through most of the afternoon becoming a more serious rain. Annie turned on the headlights and then the wipers. "We'd better find the place soon," she said. "I'm getting bored with this game."

The guidebook slid from his hand to the gritty rubber mat at his feet, and he swore. That strange tingling numbness in his knuckles and wrist again. Must be the fatigue of using the computer beginning to get to him, he thought. One of the things about middle age, you didn't spring back as fast. Next summer he'd have been on this earth half a century. Usually he didn't feel nearly that old, treated his grad students as colleagues and buddies — well, up to a point — kept up with the slang the undergraduates used and listened to the campus radio station enough to know which rock groups were in at the moment. Other times, like today, he felt every year of his life and more.

"Gas is getting low, too," Annie said. "And I sure as hell could use a drink."

He'd really set his heart on this particular inn, though, the only one within driving distance of Philly to which the guide awarded four stars. He imagined a cozy table by a fireplace, filet mignon bordelaise, a decent red wine. No other guests at this time of year. Antique furniture in their room, linen sheets on the bed, chocolates on the pillows, the sound of rain gently tapping on the windowpanes while they made love. In the night the rain would turn to snow, and in the morning they'd awake to find a fresh new world outside the casement windows.

"Let me take a look at the map, okay?" At the first spot in the road that was wide enough she pulled over, switched on the overhead light, and took the map from him.

In his mind he retraced the route they'd taken: out of King of Prussia as far as Trappe, then south onto state route 113, and then after 6.2 miles, as the guidebook directed, a right-hand turn onto a road so winding he'd joked that they'd find themselves come around full circle, and then when that road hit a crossroads and soon after became a muddy path that dead-ended in a field of cornstalks, they'd backed up and taken an unnamed and un-numbered road that his sense of direction told him had to be heading west. But they'd had no help from a setting sun, and the signs he recalled passing after the turn — Leaming, Nuneaton — weren't anywhere on the map that he could see, and now, look-ing beyond a scrabble of hedge at some cows huddling against a barn, he suddenly had the feeling that he'd been plucked bodily out of Pennsylvania and set down in some other country or time period. An oncoming truck with its high beams on made him shut his eyes, and when he opened them again, he had to blink several times before he could bring things back into focus.

"Well," Annie said, "I can't make head nor tail of it, but I sup-pose if we stay on this road, sooner or later we'll have to come to some minimal civilization where we can ask directions." She tossed the unfolded map onto the backseat before putting the car in gear and pulling onto the road. A good driver, Annie — self-confident, economical in her movements, almost masculine in the way she'd let the wheel glide casually under her fingers after making a turn instead of keeping both hands on it, as Meg did. He reached his arm across the seat back, dropping his hand onto the shoulder of Annie's jacket. The blunt-cut ends of her straight hair brushed his knuckles.

As they drove on in the rain he found himself confiding how tired he'd felt lately, the strains he'd been under: the new round of budget cuts and how they were going to cripple the department, probably irretrievably, the goddamn downsizing committee he was on, that had the potential to be the committee to end all committees, to end life as they knew it. And then, without quite knowing why — the whole purpose of this stolen weekend had been to control exactly the right place and circumstance for the revelation — he began to tell her about Meg, how in a fit of housecleaning she'd found Annie's letters behind the ancient humidifier, and at first she'd been weirdly calm about the whole thing, but then the following day she'd informed him, equally calmly, that if he wanted a divorce, fine, but if he thought she was just going to say godspeed, go start another family with your eager young professor, he could forget that, Meg would squeeze him right down to the pulp.

Annie kept on driving, not saying anything. By now the rain had slackened some, but night had truly fallen. They approached a reduced speed limit sign, passed some shabbily desolate houses, a school that looked like it had been built in the fifties sometime. But the two or three gas stations were closed, and they left the town behind them without discovering its name.

The point was, he went on, he couldn't get a divorce, not without paupering himself, but Meg wasn't going to do anything to humiliate him, she was smart enough to see it would hurt her as much as it would hurt them, it would be like killing the goose that laid the golden egg if she made a public stink that could jeopardize his career, so nothing had changed, really, so far as he and Annie were concerned . . .

"That's where you're wrong, Jim. Everything has changed."

Suddenly a neon sign loomed blearily out of the mist: a stylized palm tree with jagged fronds perched on top like a fright wig. OASIS MOTEL, said the sign, except that the T and the E were burnt out, broken front teeth. Annie turned the wheel sharply to the right, sped across the empty, potholed front lot to the office entrance. He started to protest, then silenced himself. He knew exactly what kind of place this was: smell of curry and cooking oil in the office, suspicious Pakistani proprietor, lumpy bed under orange chenille, roaches inhabiting a metal shower stall dotted with rust spots, cigarette smoke in the flimsy drapes. But if that was what she wanted . . . Annie braked the car, turned off the ignition, got out. Flexing and stretching the fingers of his right hand, he watched her open the office door and pass through it. A muscle twitched under the skin of his forearm like a tiny hyperactive frog.

5

He began to have trouble swallowing his vitamin pills, nearly choked on a deviled egg. At the bank early in December he couldn't hold the pen firmly enough to endorse his paycheck, had to step out of the line and ended up mailing the deposit in a few days later. Meg noticed that he kept stumbling, and dropping things, suggested he consider a leave of absence from the university. "Bullshit. There's nothing wrong with me," he said, although he knew there was. Stress, he thought. The subject of divorce was on hold, but always a subtext in any conversation with Meg. One afternoon he found a note stuck to the refrigerator saying she was at the hospital to have her operation, had driven herself there, would be back the next day. Annie ignored him in the department, didn't reply to the notes he left in her box. If he rang her apartment the answering machine always came on — *leave your name and number, wait for the beep* — but though he dutifully waited for the beep before he launched into his plea, she failed to return his calls.

Both boys came home for Christmas. The holiday was subdued, however: a few presents exchanged Christmas Eve, everybody sleeping late Christmas morning, roast chicken instead of turkey. In the afternoon Mike and Kevin took off to see friends in town. Meg went upstairs to do some sewing on the machine. Jim put a video into the VCR, a movie he'd looked forward to seeing, but he must have slept through it, because afterward he could not have described the plot to save his soul.

The second week of spring semester he was coming out of class and spotted Annie's tomato red beret ahead of him in the corridor. She started down the steps and he hurried after the bobbing felt; as he reached the top step he felt his leg buckle underneath him. He lurched into the wall of the stairwell, couldn't catch himself, toppled halfway down the steps and landed on his leg, breaking the tibia in two places. For some reason Jim could not fathom, the bone man who set the fracture suggested a consultation with a neurologist. Jim's health plan covered it, so what the hell, he figured, why not make the old boy happy? The neurologist ordered a bunch of tests. And when the results were all in Jim had a word — or, rather, three — for what was wrong with him: amyotrophic lateral sclerosis.

"How long?" he asked the neuron guy.

"Six months to three years."

This was February. The campus a sea of mud, the students perpetually hung over or coming down with flu, in either case surly. Only a handful had ever gotten much out of what he was trying to teach them, and he often thought that the more he drummed Renaissance drama into the few bright students who happened into his classes, the less fit they were for life in late-twentieth-century America. Why not screw it — retire and live off his disability, get around to reading the great works of literature he'd never before had time for?

Then he thought of crumbs in the bed, the insistently demanding cats, melting icicles dripping outside the bedroom window, the disagreeable comedown from Professor Mowbry to pitiful dying Jim. So he taught the following fall, not doing too badly, he thought. But he fell again, on a clear, flat sidewalk next to the business administration building, and this time broke his left wrist. Nobody in the department said anything, nobody gave him peculiar looks. In the spring semester, though, he regularly had the sensation that his tongue was a foreign object in his mouth around which he had to lecture. His right leg dragged some. Perhaps his students thought he was hitting the bottle. He found excuses to avoid committee meetings, figuring his colleagues would conclude the same thing.

By summer it was clear to him that he could not go on teaching. His speech was becoming more and more unintelligible, even to Meg, and he felt as helpless as a tourist in a country whose language he could comprehend, sort of, but not speak. His right hand and arm were nearly useless now, and the twitching and numbness were increasing on the other side. His left hand worked like a claw — no, not even as agile as a claw. He traveled to the bathroom by careening from doorjamb to bedpost to doorjamb, needed to ask Meg to button his goddamn shirt buttons, clip his toenails, help him in and out of the shower. The day he found he couldn't manage his fly zipper, he cried. He didn't go back to work in the fall.

He burned himself heating up leftovers for his lunch. Then, trying to retrieve the newspaper from the front porch, he fell once more, and this time had to have fourteen stitches in his forehead. It had become harder and harder for him to swallow his food. He assumed he'd be dead by Christmas, wondered if he'd ever see his sons again.

Without consulting him, Meg quit her job to take care of him. Strangely, those months between October and March, alone with her in the house, were the best of their marriage. Their lives retracted to their bedroom, which she'd redecorated in various shades of beige only months before. She'd carry homemade soup upstairs and help him eat it. Sitting in the creaky old rocker that had been her grandmother's, she'd read to him. Or she'd lie next to him on the bed while they watched reruns of situation comedies on a little portable TV she brought home from Kmart. One by one the three cats — Mull, Gretel, and Fog — would join them on the bed, and he didn't mind. He'd lay his heavy hand on Meg's breast, taking erotic pleasure in the rise and fall of her breathing and in the monotonous sound of the cats licking their fur. Some days Meg didn't bother to open the blinds in the morning. They'd let the telephone ring without caring who was on the other end. He could still make love. For some reason the neurons in his penis remained intact, along with — and this he often cursed — the neurons in his brain.

But he knew that his body was shrinking, especially his upper torso. He must look to her, and feel, like a concentration camp inmate. He wondered what it was like to embrace death, to have it enter your body and leave its sticky fluid presence inside you. Unwillingly and helplessly, he wept more and more often. She'd hold him, dry-eyed herself.

One day, when Meg was reading aloud from some novel or other, it occurred to him, like one of those flashes of insight that come to you after years of poring over an inscrutable manuscript, when all of a sudden you realize what the hell it *means*: His disease was the perfectly designed fate for a person who has earned his living lecturing but spent his life with his earplugs in.

Ah, crafty the gods. How they must be laughing, up there in the clouds or behind the burbling radiator, or wherever it was his personal gods hung out. He began to laugh with them. Meg looked up from her book. He laughed so much he started to cough and then to gag, upchucking onto the new deep-pile carpet. He dragged himself off the bed, and the sheet came with him, and the tray that sat on the end of it, as the cats uncoiled whip-fast and sprang into hiding. Bowls and glasses fell helter-skelter. Crash of breakage. Meg yelped. Like a serpent, the sheet wound itself around his left leg, dragged through his vomit. He grabbed for the arm of the rocking chair, missed, sprawled across

Meg's lap, rolled off onto his back. Terrible thud, wind whopped out of him. Probably yet another broken bone, or he'd lacerated himself somewhere and was already bleeding into wheat-colored deep-pile acrylic.

"This is driving me crazy," she said.

~

And when he found his voice he told her he had to get out of here, he didn't give a shit where to. With energy she seemed to have stored in the months they'd been hunkering down in the bedroom, Meg found a buyer for the house they'd lived in for a quarter of a century and bought a place on the coast of Maine, where, she told Jim, she'd always wanted to live. First he'd heard of that. Mike came home from college in May, helped his mother tag most of the family's possessions for a giant yard sale, and departed for a job on the West Coast. By the middle of June, Meg was transporting Jim east on the Garden State Parkway, across the Tappan Zee Bridge, east and north over a seemingly endless connection of interstate highways, eventually across the Piscataqua Bridge, and then some two hundred miles farther to a town he'd never been in before, never imagined existed. Meg parked in front of a building that was peeling exactly the way their house on Hawthorn Street had been peeling before he'd had the siding put on. FLAT BAY HEALTH CARE FACILITY read the sign nailed to the wall. Two friendly ladies with hair evidently cut with battery-driven hedge clippers and a burly gent who smelled of fish guts came out of the house, helped him into a wheelchair, and rolled him inside.

~

Jim sits by the plate glass window in the dayroom, overlooking a marsh where various species of birds set down on their migratory route to the south. The birds peck among the grasses in search of sustenance to maintain their long and arduous journey. He especially enjoys the black ducks and their cynical, loud, guttural *heh, heh, heh.* He feels a kinship with them. They know the meaning of life, all right, though they've been foraging in the marsh so many weeks he's beginning to suspect they'll forget to move on, get stuck in the first snowfall, have to spend the winter right here.

Meg's voice says, "Look who's come to see you."

He has just enough strength remaining in his left arm to turn the wheelchair a few inches; he sees at Meg's elbow, of all people, Professor Peter Finesilver, Oxford don. But of course, not *of all people,* but the one person he's been waiting for, he now realizes. The whole course of Jim's adult life, spent in shoving Shakespeare down the throats of boneheads in northcentral New Jersey, a fate from which he has escaped only by contracting a terminal disease, was, on that cold afternoon on Broadway, preordained in the tea leaves of Peter's politely diffident throat clearings: *It occurs to me to wonder . . . oughtn't you to consider . . .*

Jim will not try to speak. Let Peter make the apologies and voice the regrets. Peter lifts a couple of the orange plastic chairs that dot the dayroom like blotches of some hideous exotic mold and swings them over to rest in front of his wheelchair. "Hello, Jim," he says. "It's been a long time."

My God, Jim thinks, troglodyte to end all troglodytes. Ash-colored prickle-bush brows trailing off into wiry spirals, large fleshy wens on his face and neck, teeth like yellowed ivory artifacts dug out of a tomb. How did he get this way?

The Oxford don settles himself into one of the plastic chairs, trousered leg crossed over leg, and begins to talk about his current research, as though anyone on the face of the globe gives a damn. Meg, Jim sees, has backed off from this reunion. She has wandered to a card table on which lies a half-completed jigsaw puzzle and is randomly moving the pieces around.

"I've solved it," Peter says brightly. "The Digby Magdalen."

Jim feels a sound well up in his throat: fuck the Digby Magdalen, it would say if it could be interpreted as anything more than a strangled gurgle.

"It is indeed a miracle play, exactly as you posited all those years ago. And it is absolutely a coherent whole, the bridge between medieval and Renaissance drama, the missing link. The strange intermixture of references to the Virgin? It's all perfectly explained by Bernardine doctrine: the true believer becomes a 'mother' of God in the fulfillment of apostolic action. By her miracles the Magdalen comes ever closer to this divine transformation." His dark eyes behind the wire-framed spectacles glittering with excitement, Peter concludes, "The Magdalen is not confused with, but *becomes*, the Mother of God!"

There's a silence, except for some old geezer groaning in another corner of the dayroom, and then Peter leans so far forward in the orange chair that Jim imagines that in the final days of his life he's going to become infected with wens, the way you catch warts from a toad. "I did it for you, Jim," he says.

All Jim wants right now is to have the spittle wiped from his chin, the tearing blotted from the corners of his eyes. But Meg stays resolutely at the card table, fiddling with the puzzle pieces, as though neither of these men has anything to do with her.

"I'm very glad I came," Peter says quietly, and Jim can read it in his eyes: Meg slept with me. I've finally had her, Jim, and there isn't a thing you can do about it, tied into your wheelchair with a buckled webbed strap, your turkey neck encased in a surgical collar stiff as concrete.

Jim's eyes slip back to the marsh. Some little speckled birds flutter into view, gingerly alight, at some alarm rise up like bits of dust lifted by a breeze, circle to refigure their flight pattern, come down again to feed in the grasses. He feels Peter's touch on his arm, vaguely hears him utter some parting word, and soon he and Meg are gone. Take her, Jim thinks. Enjoy.

Jim recalls the kitchen in the apartment on Farnum Street. He remembers golden-haired Meg, big as a battleship, slicing into an apple, consuming the flesh and skin and stem and indigestible core, leaving on the plate only the seeds. He shuts his eyes and feels blessed sleep overtake him.

VIII

1995

THERE HADN'T yet been a frost. Inside their wire cages the tomato plants had retracted, though, like little old ladies with bone shrinkage, and the fruit on the vines seemed more exposed. Meg wrested a pair of plum tomatoes from their stem and laid them in the basket that hung from her arm. Nearby, Peter walked through dew-soaked grass, following her. "We don't get vine-ripened tomatoes at home," he said. "We have to grow them under glass."

"I know. It's not even the same vegetable."

She felt acutely the presence of the man behind her. His features had become so much more pronounced since she'd last seen him: the nose larger, the dark eyes more deeply set, the eyebrows untidy graying haymows. Wens had risen on his face and neck. His students must find him forbidding, this distinguished professor of medieval literature. And yet . . .

She turned. He was looking beyond the garden, at the retreating sea, which was leaving a mudflat in its wake. "When is it due back again?" he asked.

Meg began to explain about the tidal system, twice in, twice out, in a roughly twenty-five-hour span, but found herself floundering in the complexities of lunar pull. "Sorry, Peter. You're the one who's good at figuring out things like that, not me." She laughed, shrugging. "It's all a mystery."

"Or a miracle?" He smiled with the same shy but intimate smile that had charmed her all those years ago — intimate not in a sexual sense, precisely, but in a way that said: You and I, Meg, know a joke no one else is privy to.

"That too," she agreed, walking toward the herbs, which grew in a disorderly patch behind the tomato bed. The oregano had sprawled over the parsley and now bloomed with tiny purple flowers. Meg tore off a few branches and laid them across the tomatoes and the second-crop lettuce in the basket, and added a few sprigs of tarragon, whose stems had now become woody.

"Your garden is lovely, Meg."

"Not so lovely at this time of year." He stood so near her now that if she shifted only enough to transfer the basket to her other arm, her shoulder would touch the wool of his herringbone jacket. Fat bees hummed in the oregano. At the top of a spruce a crow cawed.

Slowly she moved away from the herb patch and said, "I don't have enough space to grow everything I'd like to. It's the trees; they don't leave me much sun. I could squeeze in one more raised bed here, I guess."

With the side of his shoe he nudged a flattish stone the size of a dessert plate. "This would be in the way."

"Wherever you dig in Maine, you find stones," she said. "They're the number one crop." She started back to the house, conscious of his footsteps following hers across the hillocky lawn, which was really only self-sown weeds and wild grasses that she periodically cut to a stubble with a hand mower.

They entered the house through the kitchen door, and she set the basket on the counter. "Why don't you sit," she said, "and keep me company while I take care of some odds and ends?"

He offered to help, but she told him no, just sit. Obediently Peter pulled a chair away from the table and settled himself while Meg emptied the lettuce and herbs into an enamel pan. She ran water into the pan, then removed a package from the refrigerator. When she'd torn open the paper wrapping she brought it to the table for him to admire the contents: fillets so fresh and thin you could almost see through them. "Lemon sole. Off the boat this morning."

"Splendid."

At the counter she began to lay the fillets onto a square of paper towel. "I'll sauté them in a little butter, nothing fancy."

He cleared his throat. "I wonder if you'd mind if I poached mine."

Poached? She pictured the delicate flesh disintegrating in an instant, swirling away into boiling water.

"It's my stomach. I can't take butter anymore, anything fried."

He looked embarrassed, and she said quickly, "Of course, Peter. But you don't need to do it yourself, I'm happy to."

Poached. She'd planned for the meal to be artlessly simple, but perfect. Now there'd be a soggy lump squatting gloomily on the white ironstone plate. Oh well, dress it up with a spray of tarragon and a lemon quarter.

Chilling was a bottle of sauterne, the best she'd been able to find in the local market. She took it out and handed it to Peter along with the corkscrew. "You still drink wine, I hope."

"Oh, yes, I still drink wine."

She thought about her twenty-second birthday dinner, the last time she'd seen him, and guessed he was thinking of that, too. Peter had brought two bottles of vintage Bordeaux as his contribution to the occasion. Claret, he called it. Peter not yet married, Meg's firstborn asleep in his crib.

Late that evening, giving in to wine-induced impulse, Meg had brought her son to the table to nurse. She knew that Peter, in the chair next to hers, could not help gazing on the baby's fuzzy head, on her own blue-veined breast swollen with milk. Her last chance to provoke a response in the gentle scholar to whom she'd become attached — he'd be on the plane back to Oxford the next day. No one else among those at the dinner table, least of all her husband, noticed a thing.

The memory of her shamelessness caused Meg some chagrin, and she busied herself rinsing lettuce while he wound the corkscrew into the cork, eased it out, and poured the pale wine into glasses she'd set before him.

She wiped her hands on a dish towel. "Cheers, Peter," she said, touching the rim of her glass to his.

"To absent friends."

"Yes," she replied, "to absent friends." With her glass she returned to the counter.

Peter was Jim's friend before he was hers, of course. Impressed by his prestige, Jim would bring the visiting scholar back to their apartment for drinks after the Thursday afternoon seminar, and presently she'd invite him to stay for potluck. By chance she'd have cooked something a little special that day. Or maybe not exactly by chance. Soon her whole week began and ended with Thursdays, even though she was pregnant with Jim's child, and in the spring semester nursing Jim's son.

After Peter returned to England the men's interests took different turns: Jim's lurching into Tudor drama, where he calculated the jobs were, Peter's wending into linguistics and theology. Meg was the one who assumed the task of keeping in touch. Except that it wasn't a task. She wrote the offhand, chatty letters responding to Peter's, only once in a while slipping in some small self-revelation, like a wrapped candy tucked as a surprise into a lunch bag. About as often she'd receive something like that from him, a minute confession woven as if by accident into his amusing observations on a concert he'd attended, or some international intrigue, or the commotion among his colleagues when a certain fourteenth-century leechbook inexplicably vanished from the Bodleian. Even after Peter wed, the occasional letters back and forth across the Atlantic continued. Twenty-seven years, and still her heart leapt a little whenever a blue air letter with his curious hooked handwriting on it arrived in the mail.

From the kitchen table Peter said, "You haven't had an easy time of it, Meg."

She would not, she'd already decided, reveal to Peter that the marriage had been as good as dead well before Jim's puzzling symptoms began to manifest themselves. Instead, she sat at the table with her wineglass and talked about the decision to quit her job, sell the house, and move up here, once looking after her husband at home with the help of hired students was no longer a way of life either she or Jim cared to go on with. She'd always dreamed of living near the sea. The inside of a nursing home — as long as it's decent, what does it matter where it is?

"But will you be all right? Financially, I mean."

She pushed her flyaway hair back from her forehead and explained that money wasn't a problem: Jim's disability pension was relatively generous, the kids' educations paid for. They had a nest egg, investments that had done surprisingly well over the years. No fortune, certainly, but enough for Meg to be comfortable, enough to pay for the nursing home until . . .

"Would you like to see him?" Meg asked, still not altogether sure she understood the reason Peter had rented a car and driven the three hundred miles north from Boston, where his conference was about to convene.

"Will he know me?"

"Do you mean, does he still have his mind?"

Peter found a crumb on the tablecloth and rolled it between his fingers.

"The sorry part is that he does. He won't be able to talk to you, though. Look, Peter, if you'd rather not . . . I didn't mention to him that you were coming."

He smiled slightly, his eyes cast down on the tablecloth. "That leaves it up to me, then."

"Well, we can play it by ear."

Fog, the arthritic gray tabby, padded in from the living room where he'd been napping and wound himself around Meg's legs. She got up and let the cat out the kitchen door, which still had its screen in place. Soon Meg would have to summon the ambition to haul the storm doors and windows out of the cellar, wash and install them. Other maintenance jobs also needed attention. The dripping hot water tap in the laundry room. A finicky switch in the upstairs hall. Leaves clogging gutters and drainpipes. Maybe Peter . . . But no, not dressed like that. He wouldn't have work clothes in the small carry-on satchel he'd brought with him, which now reposed on the bed in the spare room upstairs.

Neither of them had so far spoken of Enid, the wife he mentioned in his letters only rarely. Because Meg had been rattling on so much about herself, and about Jim, she decided she ought, for politeness's sake, to bring Enid into the conversation. "Your wife. She didn't think of coming with you to the conference?"

Peter smiled. "I'm afraid she's far too busy with her work at the moment."

"She's a lawyer, right?"

He'd removed his wire-framed eyeglasses and was cleaning them with his pocket handkerchief. They'd left raw-looking dents on the bridge of his nose, as if he'd been pinched in a vice. "She's a partner in a large firm of solicitors. They do mostly corporate work."

"In Oxford?"

"Oh, no," he said, returning the glasses to his face and the handkerchief to his pocket. "In London, in the City."

One by one Meg began to transfer the draining fillets onto a fresh piece of paper towel. "She must find the commute a hassle."

"Enid lives in North London. She has a flat in Hampstead."

"Oh," Meg replied. If he had any feelings one way or the other about this coolly practical arrangement, Meg couldn't tell. Perhaps she was missing a cue that an English person would immediately have picked up on.

"We go on holidays together. We're planning a walking tour of Northumberland next spring."

"That sounds nice."

"You can still find bits of Hadrian's Wall." He paused. "Little heaps of brick, mostly. To see them you have to invade suburban housing estates, go bursting into people's gardens."

She laughed, at the same time wondering whether he was going to reveal more about the situation with Enid. When he didn't continue, she said, "Maybe you'd like a shower before we eat. Would you? Or no, a bath. Englishmen take baths."

While she sliced tomatoes and sectioned a lemon and put the potatoes on to boil, she listened to the bathwater running overhead. She tried not to think about Peter in the lion-footed porcelain tub, rubbing her clear glycerine soap over his body.

She glanced at the electric wall clock above the refrigerator. Right now they'd be feeding Jim his soft supper, most of which would dribble from his slack jaw and soil his bib. Then they'd lift him onto the bedpan to produce his few smelly pellets. Jim had bedded a goodly number of his female graduate students and at least one untenured faculty member, for years lying in his teeth to Meg and getting away with it. Still, she supposed not even he deserved to end his days this way.

∼

After dinner, against the chill that had crept up from the misty bay, Meg jacked the thermostat up a couple of degrees and built a fire in the fireplace. Her first fire of the season, she told Peter, sweeping up bits of bark and fungus that had fallen from the logs onto the hearth. They sat on the sofa, one cushion's space between them, and drank decaf and port. She talked about her boys, Kevin doing relief work in El Salvador, Mike traipsing around Nepal on a year off between college and graduate school. Maybe Peter found it strange that they'd taken off to remote regions of the globe when their father was dying. Actually, it hadn't seemed like defection when, one after the other, they departed: Kevin born with a passion for curing the world's ills, perhaps inherited from Meg's missionary great-grandparents; Mike's wandering a kind of family joke, as a child forever going astray in supermarkets and shopping malls. With her thumbnail Meg traced a hairline crack in her demitasse cup. Now that she thought about it, though . . . perhaps it wasn't such a coincidence that both were so far out of reach now.

To get off that subject she told Peter about joining a church choir in town. For ages she'd been wanting an opportunity to sing choral music; somehow she hadn't found the time when she was working. The church people were nice, a bit like a family.

Did she miss her job? Peter asked.

Well, writing résumés had its moments. You could think of it as inventing people's lives, like a novelist or a psychotherapist. Or God. But most of the clients would never do justice to the identities she'd conjured for them. Meg set her cup on the tray. Poor souls destined to fail even before they passed through the frosted door of Life Designs, Inc.

Why? Hard to tell, in an objective way. Once they'd held responsible positions, successfully applied for mortgages, managed to keep families together. You couldn't miss the doom in their gray faces, though, in the stiff way they held themselves, arms crossed over their chests, fingers clutching their jacket sleeves, dazedly watching the tropical fish swim round the tank. Rubber heels digging into Life Designs' stained carpet.

Sometimes, she told Peter, the ghosts of those clients used to invade her dreams. They'd shake their laser-printed lives in her face, chase her along dark, mazelike corridors, their huge shadows nearly catching up with her. Thankfully, she rarely had those dreams anymore. No, she had to admit she didn't miss her job.

She got up to stoke the fire, and Peter poured a little more golden port into their glasses. He took a cloth handkerchief from his trouser pocket and wiped the stickiness from the neck of the bottle and from his fingers.

The radiator pipes gurgled. Meg began to talk about the weird plumbing in the house, installed in a haphazard way by amateurs half a century ago. She told him how the pipes had frozen and burst last winter, flooding the downstairs so that she'd had to retreat to the second floor with the cats. She'd felt like Noah's wife, she said, spinning out the yarn, making a joke of her inexperience in managing an antiquated house on her own. Her face was flushed, she knew, with drink and the heat of the fire.

In the silence that now fell over them, the clock on the mantel began to strike the hour of nine. "For me," Peter said, soon after it ceased chiming, "it's two in the morning." At the same moment they set their empty glasses down on the tray, and his knuckles bumped the underside of her wrist. Attentively they gazed at one another, Peter's haymow brows seeming to take on an agitated life of their own. She rose to her feet.

"Peter, I don't want to put you on the spot. I'll simply tell you that my bedroom is the one at the far end of the hall, and if you should feel chilly or lonely or anything . . ."

Meg didn't wait for a reply. She crossed the Oriental rug and a bare stretch of waxed hardwood and mounted the steps, leaving the port bottle uncorked and a heap of partially burned scraps of log still smoking in the fireplace.

～

He did come, after she'd decided he wasn't going to, and lifted the quilt so he could climb into bed beside her. "Meg," he said softly, "I don't have . . . I wasn't prepared to . . ."

"It's been taken care of," Meg whispered.

Now she and Peter began to make love, twenty-seven years and four months after that sweet, urgent farewell kiss in the back stairwell of the Farnum Street apartment building, Meg's breasts leaking painfully through her crushed-velvet dress, her husband at the table holding forth on the *Regularis Concordia,* full of Peter's wine, oblivious. How close she'd come then to running down the steps after the gentle Englishman and folding herself into his luggage, and allowing herself to be transported to an England she knew like the back of her hand from reading Katherine Mansfield and Virginia Woolf. But Kevin's wail dragged her back inside the apartment, and everywhere were perilously stacked dishes to be washed, still encrusted with the remains of coq au vin and cake.

On Peter's back she felt bumps and small scarred depressions, where there must have been minor surgery, and she knew he was feeling the folds on her stomach and the layered flesh that skidded awkwardly under his caressing palms. But how very good it was, this loving. Inside her, his mouth at her breast, he said in a ragged voice, "Such a long time to wait, my Meg."

After he slept she still held him, listening to his slow breathing and to the tide, now high, sucking at marsh grass. *My Meg. My Meg.*

He wheezed a little, drew out of her arms, and turned himself over — careful, even in his sleep, not to encroach on her share of the bed — snorted once, fell into a deeper slumber.

Suddenly she remembered rescuing from the trash, that birthday night, the corks from the vintage claret. What had become of them afterward?

∾

Meg awoke at first light, pulled on a sweater and pants quietly so as not to wake him, and went downstairs. In the kitchen she found that before coming to bed he'd carried out the tray. She wondered whether he'd been anguishing over what they were about to do as he corked the port, as he rinsed the glasses and demitasse cups and put them upside down in the drainer. Or perhaps he'd been completely calm, with nothing more troubling on his mind than the duty to be a helpful guest, giving her time to change her mind if she wanted to. She let the cats in and fed them and then, filled with an energy she wasn't sure what to do with, went outside.

Over the crunchy grass she walked down the slope to the water's edge. Tide on its way out again, the rising sun casting an orangy pink shimmer on pools that lingered in wet sand, stippled gray clouds above the horizon like stripes on an animal. How sad that the sunrise was wasted: Peter was sleeping through it. In the woods behind her a raven shrieked *quork, quork,* setting off a chain reaction of *quorks* from spruce to spruce.

Her muscles itched to be doing something. She turned and climbed back up the slope, skirted the house, yanked open the shed door. From a box of moldy garden gloves, the finger ends nothing but fraying holes, she chose a couple at random and took a shovel from among the tangle of tools that leaned against the wall. She'd disturbed a spiderweb. Enough light reached the inside of the shed so that she could watch the disconcerted spider scramble up the planks.

Leaving the door ajar, Meg forced the mud-stiffened gloves onto her hands and toted the shovel around to the vegetable garden. It shouldn't take long to move that flat stone. She could have coffee brewing and muffins in the oven before he came downstairs. With the tip of the shovel she began to lift chunks of turf from the edge of the stone, but as she was doing so she discovered that its diameter was wider than she'd assumed, more like a dinner plate than a dessert plate. Crabgrass and chickweed had matted over the surface several inches all around the circumference. When she had that stripped away, she tried to work the shovel blade down under the stone in order to pry it up, but the blade clanked against rock. Nothing budged; the resistance jarred the bones in her forearms and set her teeth on edge. The stone must not be flat, after all, but have some depth to it. She moved the blade away from the exposed stone half a foot or so and tried again, forcing the blade down through grass by pressing her heel hard against the shoulder. This time she was able to move some soil, which, being solid clay, stuck to the blade in clumps.

After four or five more shovelfuls, sweat started to gather in her armpits and her heart was beating faster. Not as young as I used to be, she thought. The rock that had begun to emerge seemed to be granite, coarse-grained in texture, unevenly rounded, a pinkish color. Chips of quartz or mica embedded in the granite glinted in the sunlight. This stone was clearly a lot larger than she'd suspected, even a few minutes ago.

Meg pushed the sleeves of her sweater up to the elbows, then circled the stone and moved another half dozen shovelfuls of the dense gray soil, rested awhile, moved yet another half dozen. She leaned on the handle, her chest heaving. This was going to be some rock.

By the time she had the whole thing exposed, more than an hour later, it sat complacently in a pit maybe a yard deep. Streaks of gray dirt covered her arms and the front of her sweater. Her khakis were filthy, and so were her sneakers. She stripped off the mismatched gloves and tossed them aside.

Peter, dressed in fresh white shirt and herringbone jacket, came strolling over the hillocky lawn toward the garden. "Good morning," he said. "I wondered what happened to you."

"Rats. I was going to have coffee and homemade muffins all ready for you."

"That's a big stone," he said, looking down into the pit. "How are you going to get it out of the hole?"

She thought for a moment and then began to laugh. "Damned if I know."

"What you need is a winch."

"Fresh out of winches, I'm afraid." She picked up the shovel. "Come on back to the house, and I'll give you some breakfast."

～

Water dripped down the nape of her neck. With her left hand she rubbed her hair with a towel, with her right she pulled on a moccasin. Peter was sitting on the edge of the bed, which he must have made before coming downstairs in search of her. "I haven't watched a woman dress in longer than I can remember," he said.

She didn't answer right away. Then, "I'm sorry it couldn't have been a younger and more beautiful woman to break your . . ." Fast? Vow? ". . . whatever it was."

". . . Whatever it was." Without a smile he said, "I liked this woman fine."

She dried her hair some more, threw the towel over the bed rail, combed her fingers through the damp strands. "Every morning I drive into town to see him," she said. "He'll wonder what's wrong if I don't show up."

"You must go, then."

"Are you going to come?"

"Would you like me to?"

She sat next to him on the bed. "It's not a lot of fun, Peter. He can't talk. He tries to, but all that comes out are baby sounds. *Gaa, gaa.* And that frustrates him terribly, of course. Probably what he's trying to say is: Why the hell don't you just shoot me in the head and get it over with?"

Peter took her hand, which was raw and blistered from the digging, and wove his fingers in with hers. She'd stopped wearing her wedding band. The back of Peter's hand bore a couple of liver spots, as well as some spidery graying hairs sprouting from his knuckles. He wasn't wearing a ring, either, but then, she had an idea that wedding bands for men weren't as common in England as they were here.

"And," she went on, "after last night, you might feel uncomfortable, as if you'd taken advantage of him, of his being sick, though you certainly can't be blamed for what we did, it was my idea, and — "

"Blame isn't the issue." He said that gently, almost regretfully.

"Peter, I swore to myself I wasn't going to tell you this, but I have to now."

"What?" She hesitated, and he said again, "What is it, Meg?"

"Jim cheated on me. Quite a bit. Before he got sick."

He looked down at their intertwined hands. "Are you saying that what you wanted was to even the score?"

She was shocked he'd think that. "No, Peter. What I want is for you to understand the whole situation. Because it feels wrong to keep secrets from you, because —" But how could she come right out and tell him that she loved him, without ruining everything? She withdrew her hand from his grasp and stood. Damned if she'd humiliate herself by weeping in front of him.

"Because Jim and I were friends?"

"Yes, that's it," she said, her throat constricted. "I'd better go."

He followed her downstairs and out to the dooryard. After a moment's confusion, sorting out which was the driver's side of her little compact and which the passenger's, Peter got in and shut the door.

❧

At some indefinable time between their entering the kitchen and leaving the house again, the sky had become overcast, threatening rain. The trip to town was about six miles, first on a dirt road along the narrow peninsula, the colorless bay sometimes visible through the trees, then a turn onto a paved numbered route that passed some fields and barns, crossed an iron bridge. Conversation along the way was deliberately bland: How many people live in the village? How do they earn their livings? Meg could have bitten her tongue for having told Peter about Jim's screwing around, which had served no purpose but to make this expedition even more awkward than it would have been otherwise. And she wished she'd eaten something, filthy though she'd been, rather than gone right upstairs to shower after she'd fixed Peter's breakfast. Her gut felt queasy. She'd developed a headache that was like a narrow-gauge drill bit intermittently entering her skull above her left eye.

Meg pulled into the parking lot in front of the nursing home, and they got out. The home, a white wooden structure with striped awnings, had been a private house in the days when sardine canneries had brought moderate prosperity to the town. Now it looked as defeated as the industry that had funded it, the awnings tattered by winter storms and the wood needing a coat of paint. Still, Meg told Peter as they walked up the steps, the aides were kind and competent, and in spite of its age and makeshift repairs, the place was kept pretty clean. You couldn't hope for much more than that.

They found Jim in the dayroom, in a wheelchair parked near a window that overlooked the marsh. She saw him now through Peter's eyes: his hair not exactly gray, but faded and much thinner, the mouth drooping, spittle leaking from one corner. Tall as ever, but the muscles gone as slack as his mouth, so that he had to have a strap buckled around his shrunken torso, as if he were a dummy stuffed with rags, and his neck propped inside a surgical collar. The sweatshirt and jogging pants he wore were easier than regular clothes for the aides to manage when they dressed and undressed him. How the irony in that must rankle, since Jim had prided himself on his fitness. As if it were her own, she felt Jim's shame. She should never have brought Peter here.

He carried two chairs across the scuffed tile floor, which was laid out like a checkerboard, and set them in front of Jim's wheelchair. "Hello, Jim," he said, settling himself into one of them.

Jim did not try to speak. Maybe it was Meg's imagination, but his expression seemed wary — frightened, even.

"It's been a long time," Peter said. The near-echo of what he'd murmured to Meg, his tongue licking at her nipple, made her wince and turn away. She almost would have preferred him to exclaim, "You look grand, Jim," and clap him on his bony shoulder.

She didn't take the chair next to Peter's. Instead she stood at a card table on which lay a jigsaw, half completed. The picture was of a whitewashed cottage, yellow roses climbing a trellis along the left-hand border. Distractedly she chose a puzzle piece and turned it this way and that, trying to fit it into gaps on the trellis. In a far corner of the room an ancient gentleman moaned in his sleep.

Peter began to tell Jim about a paper he'd recently completed, a problem he thought he'd solved. "The Digby Magdalen," she heard him say, and she recalled that when he was a graduate student Jim had written a seminar paper on a play about Mary Magdalen, which had given him fits. For some reason he'd expected Peter to help him with the project, and resented it when Peter went on devoting himself to his own research instead. She looked up and saw that Jim's pale eyes had begun to water at the corners. If Peter weren't here, she'd have lifted an edge of the cloth diaper knotted around Jim's neck and wiped them for him, and the slobber at his mouth. His feet, in their fuzzy bed socks, stirred. A kind of gurgle, impossible to interpret, came from deep in his throat.

. . . indeed a miracle play, Peter was saying *. . . absolutely a co-*

herent whole . . . bridge between medieval and Renaissance . . .
Bernardine doctrine . . . by her miracles the Magdalen comes ever
closer to divine transformation . . . is not confused with, but becomes *the Mother of God . . .*

Like an egg balanced on end, Jim's head wobbled at the top of
his stiff collar. His left hand lifted from the arm of the chair,
flopped down again. Meg began to move toward them, diago-
nally across black and white squares.

Peter leaned forward in the chair. Mysteriously he said, "I did
it for you, Jim." His voice seemed to drop a little. "I'm very glad I
came." For a horrifying moment Meg thought he was going to
confide in Jim what had transpired in the upstairs bedroom. And
perhaps he had — with his smile. Gently he touched the sleeve of
Jim's sweatshirt and said, "Good-bye, friend."

Out at the car, Meg discovered that she still held the yellow jigsaw piece in her hand. She placed it on the dashboard, thinking
she'd return it the following day, and turned the key in the ignition. They didn't speak at all on the way home.

∼

Peter laid his chicken sandwich on his plate and said, "Did you
ever consider divorcing him?"

"When I found out he'd been sleeping around?" She rose to
take from the refrigerator the bowl of fruit salad left from the
previous night's dinner. Overnight the cut fruit had released its
juice, and the banana turned dark and soggy. She sat and
spooned some of the salad onto her plate. "Sure I considered it."

"You could have married again," Peter said, examining his half-
eaten sandwich.

"There wasn't anyone around I wanted to marry." Their
glances met, then she looked out the window at speckled yellow
birch leaves drifting down in a light breeze. Might be going to
rain soon.

"Anyway, it would have been so hard, Peter. So painful to drag all those bitter feelings into the open, into a court of law. I figured that having Jim gone for good wouldn't be that much different from the way life had been for me for years. Whether he'd spent his evening in a carrel writing a journal article or in someone's bed, the effect was the same."

Meg ate a spoonful of the fruit salad. "Then, around the time I'd gotten used to the idea of Jim's girlfriend, the odd symptoms began. The first thing was, he had trouble holding a pen tightly enough to write with it. That hand and arm would twitch, like a cat convinced it has fleas. I suggested his problem might be psychological — maybe he needed a rest from doing so much scholarship. Bullshit, he said. Next he fell down a flight of stairs after a lecture and had to be brought home in an ambulance. Fractured his leg in two places."

"I remember your writing about the broken leg."

"Even then I didn't suspect anything was seriously wrong. People do stumble and fall, even healthy people."

"They do," Peter said.

"He spent six weeks hobbling around on crutches. During that time he started to have trouble swallowing, would gag or choke on things. Stew meat, vitamin pills, even oatmeal. Finally his doctor made him see a neurologist."

One of the cats was mewing outside the screen door, but Meg ignored it. "And then we knew. After that, there was no question of divorce."

Peter nodded.

She rose from the table and scraped her plate into the compost bucket. "Peter," she said abruptly, "when your wife decided to take a flat in Hampstead, did divorce cross your mind?"

It took him a moment to collect his thoughts. "I understood from the start how important Enid's work was to her. She tried living in Oxford for a year, as we'd agreed, but found it too confining. Her right to a career was part and parcel of our bargain."

Bargain. A strange way to express the concept of marriage, but accurate enough, Meg supposed.

"I felt obliged to honor it."

"And you still do."

"Yes. I still do."

After a silence, during which he attended to his sandwich, she said, "Is your paper really about Mary Magdalen?"

The question seemed to startle him. "Of course. Why do you ask?"

"What did you mean when you told Jim you wrote it for him?"

"Meg," he said, "let's talk about the hole."

"What hole?"

"The hole with the stone in it, where you want to put in another bed."

"Oh, that hole."

He smiled, and his haymow brows lifted. "I was thinking about it on the way back from seeing Jim. Do you happen to have a crowbar?"

She'd inherited a bunch of old tools rusting away in the shed when she'd bought the house. "I think I recall seeing one. Maybe even two."

"Let's have a go."

∼

He washed up the lunch dishes, spilling a certain amount of water on the linoleum floor in front of the sink, while she rooted around upstairs to find something he could wear. Hanging in Mike's closet was a pair of corduroys he'd worn before he took his great growth spurt — heaven only knew why they'd been preserved, even through the move to Maine — and in the ragbag she found a flannel shirt of Jim's, out at the elbows, that she'd been saving to rip into dustcloths.

Arrayed in these hand-me-downs, Peter was a comical sight. The threadbare corduroys came only to his shins, and she'd already removed the buttons from the shirt, so she had to safety-pin him into it. The sleeves, way too long, dangled over his hands until he turned them up. She got out the camera, in case she ever needed to blackmail him, she said. But as she watched him trundle the wheelbarrow over hillocks toward the woodpile, she thought there was something indefinably erotic about seeing him in her son's and husband's clothing.

Meg took a picture of him loading logs into the barrow, then set the camera on a stump, propped on a piece of kindling, so that the time-delay mechanism could capture the two of them together. She came next to him and put her arm around his waist, hugging him to her, feeling the soft, worn flannel under her fingers, and told him to smile. They held still, watching the little red light blink, waiting for the shutter to slide open. If only it never would, if only they could stand that way forever. But the shutter opened, hesitated for a fraction of a second, and slid shut, and the automatic advance whirred. "One more?" she asked. Too late: he'd turned and was heaving a log into the barrow.

After Peter dumped the pile of logs near the hole, he positioned two fat ones, split side down, next to the rim and picked up one of the long crowbars they'd found in the shed. "Right," he said. "With the crowbars we're going to lever up the rock as high as we can, using these logs as fulcrums. Then I'll nudge a log into the hole with my foot, and while you steady the rock, I'll use my crowbar to shove the log under. If we can get enough logs under the rock to raise it to the surface, then all we need to do is roll it off."

"*If*," she said. "Okay, let's give it a try."

Easier said than done. The stone weighed a ton, and it wanted to wobble off the forked end of her crowbar, especially when Peter used his to maneuver the log in the hole. Nevertheless, he eventually succeeded in forcing the first log beneath the stubborn granite. The stone lurched sideways and upward about an inch, and Peter, red in the face, let out a cheer.

"This time, I'll hold the rock, and you do the maneuvering," he said. He repositioned the fulcrum logs, and again they levered the granite upward. Unfortunately, the log she kicked into the hole turned out to be too big, and she had a devil of a time manipulating it. Meanwhile, Peter, struggling to raise the rock higher with his crowbar so her job wouldn't be so hard, became even redder in the face. Please God, let him not burst an artery, she prayed. At last she managed to wedge the log more or less underneath, the granite seemed a little higher, and they both cheered.

"If only we had a third person to work the logs in while we held the crowbars," she said, "it would be a piece of cake. Almost." Both of them, probably, pictured Jim in town in the nursing home, drooling into his bib.

"We can do it," Peter said. "We've made a good start already. We have to go slow, take rests, spell each other holding up the rock."

Together they developed a knack and a rhythm. Circling the rock with the fulcrums, they jammed the logs one by one under the rock and on top of the ones below; little by little the heap of logs Peter had dumped by the hole shrank. There were some setbacks, when the logs under the rock would suddenly shift and catapult it into the clay wall of the hole, and they'd have to ram it toward the center again, Peter grunting and Meg muttering swearwords. Nevertheless, gradually the rock's shoulders, and then middle, emerged.

"It's working, Peter. They ought to give you the Nobel Prize in physics for this."

He smiled as though he'd finished making his acceptance

speech and was modestly acknowledging the crowd's applause. "How long do you think it's been buried?" he asked.

"Oh, roughly since the last ice age."

The higher the rock rose the better they got at weaving the logs in beneath it, outwitting the rough-skinned, clay-encrusted, bull-headed enemy. At last it was entirely out of the hole, squatting on top of what seemed like the best part of a cord of logs, its bottom surface level with the terrain.

Meg flopped down on the grass they'd trampled, feeling almost the same exhausted euphoria as after the births of her babies. Peter took off his ratty garden gloves and mopped his forehead with the handkerchief he'd stowed in Mike's pocket. His graying hair was stuck to his head, drenched in sweat. He removed his eyeglasses and wiped them, too. "That rock must be the size of a washtub," he said.

"I beg your pardon. That rock is at least the size of a dinghy."

Nearsightedly he blinked at it. "Dory."

"Tugboat."

"That rock," he declared, hooking his eyeglasses over his ears, "is the size of the bloody *Queen Mary*."

She loved him so much it felt like a disease you could die of, no less hopeless than Jim's. "You're leaving tomorrow, aren't you," she blurted.

He stuffed the handkerchief into a pants pocket and sat beside her on the grass. "Friday is the day I give my paper," he said quietly.

You couldn't get somebody else to deliver it for you? she wanted to ask. You couldn't say what the hell, screw the goddamn paper? But if anything like that were possible for him, he'd have to suggest it himself. She rolled over and pressed her face into the crook of her arm so that if she were to weep he wouldn't see the tears. After a while Peter laid his hand on the back of her work shirt, his fingers light as a leaf falling. "Are you all right?" he asked.

"I'm not having a heart attack, if that's what you mean."

"I don't know what to say, Meg."

"Then don't say anything."

The rain that had been threatening since late morning began as a finely sieved drizzle. Soon Peter stood and brushed mud and dried grass clippings from Mike's corduroys. They returned the crowbars to the shed and went into the house.

～

A week after Peter drove away in the rental car, Meg pulled the tomato plants out of their bed, cut up the stalks with kitchen shears, and added them to the compost.

The following day the minister of the church where she sings in the choir arrived in a pickup, along with two parishioners. With little effort the three men toppled the big rock off the hole. "Which way?" they asked, and when Meg replied that she didn't care, they rolled it toward the seaward side of the lawn, which they chose not for aesthetic reasons but because the land sloped in that direction. The rock came to rest against a knot of skinny stumps belonging to an alder that Meg had sawed down the previous spring, near the edge of the woods.

Her helpers rescued the logs from the hole and restacked them on the woodpile. They shoveled the clumps of clay back into the hole and topped it up with soil from a hill of loam, now nourishing canes of wild raspberry, that had been trucked in the previous year for her first raised beds. Meg could hardly bear to watch the operation, but felt it would be ungracious not to stay outside until they were finished and afterward offer them coffee. To her relief, the men didn't ask who'd helped her lift the rock. Might as well have been done by snapping her fingers and saying abracadabra.

Every time she passes a window on the garden side of the house Meg's eye snags on the rock. It looks naked and forlorn, sitting there on frosty grass. In the spring she'll plant a clump of daylilies next to it, maybe splurge on a mugho pine to nestle up against its rough pink surface.

Before leaving the country Peter wrote her a brief letter on hotel stationery. It was raining in Boston, he said. He'd lost his umbrella somewhere, absentmindedly left it under his chair in the conference room where he read his paper, or perhaps in the taxi afterward. In all probability, he'd encounter rain when he landed in London, too. "I expect," he wrote in his tiny, hooked, nearly illegible hand, "it will be a long while until I see the sun again." Since that note she hasn't heard from him.

The snapshots came back from York Photo Labs. The one of Peter at the woodpile is a little blurry and poorly framed — she'd been overeager. The one of the two of them, shot by time delay, could be any middle-aged couple on a camping holiday: the woman's hair awry, the man's face mostly in shadow. No details (the safety pins on the flannel shirt, for instance) visible to anyone who didn't know they were there. She'd ordered a double set of prints, but won't be sending the extra pair on to him, probably.

Jim's still hanging on in the nursing home, a little weaker each day. Gradually he seems to be withdrawing to the private place where people go before they die. Yes, she did remember to take the jigsaw piece from the car's dashboard back to the dayroom. Turned out it wasn't part of the rose trellis, but the feathers of some yellow bird — oriole? — in the upper-right-hand corner of the puzzle.

Unaccountably, as the year winds down, Meg finds her spirits lifting. Maybe her disease isn't a fatal one, after all. Yesterday Mike telephoned from Kathmandu to say he'll definitely be home by Christmas. She's looking forward to it.